Death of the Party

Also by Leela Cutter:

Who Stole Stonehenge?
Murder After Tea-time

Death of the Party

Leela Cutter

St. Martin's Press / New York

DEATH OF THE PARTY. Copyright © 1985 by Leela Cutter. All rights reserved. Printed in the United States of America. No part of this book may be used or reproduced in any manner whatsoever without written permission except in the case of brief quotations embodied in critical articles or reviews. For information, address St. Martin's Press, 175 Fifth Avenue, New York, N.Y. 10010.

Library of Congress Cataloging in Publication Data

Cutter, Leela.
    Death of the party.

    I. Title.
PS3553.U86D4   1985   813'.54   85–10066
ISBN 0–312–18871–4

First Edition

10 9 8 7 6 5 4 3 2 1

For Kathy, who knows a thing or two
about style and friendship

Death of the Party

1

THE HARVEST MOON was well over the horizon, gleaming amber on the soft leather of the convertible's interior. Max had left the top down and the autumnal scent of wet leaves flowed over the edge of the windscreen, but he was warm in the cockpit's pocket of still air. His pulse was faster than normal, his senses especially receptive to the night around him. At the moment it was enough just to be alive, or nearly enough. It was always this way at the beginning of a gambit.

He flexed his wrist, exposing his Rolex Oyster from under the perfect amount of cuff. Timing was such a vital aspect of camouflage; slip in unobtrusively, never late, never early. He patted his breast pocket out of habit; the miniaturized camera with special high-speed film could barely be noticed beneath the impeccable cut of his dinner jacket.

In the cone of his headlamp beams he saw the tall wrought-iron spears of the Victorian fence that encompassed the estate. Most nights they would have posed an impenetrable barrier; but now a quick racing downchange into second swept him through the open gates and up the long expanse of drive to Castleberry, one of the grandest houses in the heart of Mayfair. The barriers around the house, formidable in earlier reconnoiterings, seemed to evaporate in the night.

He fishtailed to a stop as an elderly Rolls-Royce Phaeton pulled away from the sweep of the portico. With a silly-ass grin he vaulted out of the car without using the door, amusing neither of the liveried footmen. They stood to either side of a pair of immense doors that wouldn't have looked out of place at the Vatican.

"Love your wig," he snickered at one of the servants, running his eyes down the man's seventeenth-century lace-fronted jacket, pantaloons, and chased silver accessories. Leave it to Gwenna Hardcastle to keep her servants in brocades and hosiery as appropriate backdrop to her own imperial regalia. Every night was fancy dress for the Queen of Historical Romance.

"Put it in the barn, would you?" Max said.

The footman nodded a fractional increment. "Very good, sir." The remaining servant stood expressionless as the motor purred to life and the car disappeared around the side of the house.

Max removed his slim gold-plated cigarette case from his pocket, extracting a Sobranie special blend. One servant down, one to go; even odds or better. He tapped the cigarette end on the case as he surveyed the scene. The tedious labouring of a string quartet bored its way through the open portals, overlaid by the chink of crystal and the endless buzz of cocktail chat. He decided to wait for the next limousine, now coming up the drive, before making his move.

But a fresh possibility appeared out of the shadow of a fluted column. She was tall and slim in a slightly clinging number that revealed less skin than was usual these days. With dark, tousled hair under an old-fashioned lace shawl, she was unselfconsciously sexy. And, he noted in the way she pulled her wrap closer around her, somehow vulnerable.

He approached her with the bouncy chagrin of a sportsman recovering a lost pony. "There you are!" he exclaimed, making certain that his voice carried to the door. "Been beating the bush for you."

"I beg your pardon?" came her frosty response.

He tucked a hand through the crook of her arm and led her towards the door, exploiting the element of surprise. "Been waiting long?" He felt her first tug of resistance and overcame it as he nattered on. "Your date's going to be a bit late, I'm afraid. He asked me to look after you till he arrived."

"*He* did?"

They stopped at the door. The doorman stiffened to attention, a fistful of invitations in one gloved hand. Moment of truth, Max thought. He heard the squeal of brakes as the limo pulled up, idling as its occupants waited impatiently to have the doors opened. "Sir. Madame." The doorman had only half an eye on them.

"Come on, darling, go along with the fun," Max coaxed with a wink, feeling a small bead of sweat on his forehead, the first premonition of failure. He could see in her eyes that he had made a mistake.

"Oh, all right," she finally said and extracted the invitation from a minuscule purse. "Darling," she added, with strong ironic emphasis.

As they passed through the doors, flashbulbs popped in their faces. Max smiled graciously down at the aging society photographer he'd seen at a tony bash last month. He squeezed the hand that held the camera, murmuring, "Take another shot, luv, you didn't get my best side." The photographer giggled, but turned his attention to the next batch of arrivals. Max's companion practically dislocated his shoulder tugging him out of the foyer.

As they entered the ballroom he felt like a pet guppy dumped from his comfortable bowl into the vastness of the open sea. Columns and galleries soared to the rosy-hazed firmament where crystal chandeliers hovered like alien spacecraft. Behind the starchy-looking quartet, red brocade waterfalls cascaded out of the heights and bracketed the larger-than-life oils of various turgid scenes.

"I never trust anybody who hangs wreaths on her busts," his companion remarked, rolling her eyes at a bedecked marble bust of Napoleon.

But Max was impressed. "Amazing what can be achieved with cubic cash. Shall we dance?" The strings of the orchestra tripped playfully around them as they gently whirled. Max could hear the creak of shoe leather and the rustle of silk as couples danced past. Bits of conversation as well.

"Sheep? Baaing on the phone? Poor Gwenna must be—"

". . . and it's anything but her usual exclusive affair."

"She was very odd when I rang her up yesterday. Didn't seem to recognise my voice!"

"You've got one ear to the ground, haven't you?" This last his partner whispered in his ear.

"Checking the pulse of the party," was his suave reply.

"What's that lump in your breast pocket—or are you just happy to see me?"

He grinned. "A spy camera, of course."

"On Her Majesty's Secret Service? You certainly look the part."

"Then I'm doing okay."

"It got you in the door. Oh goodie, the music's stopped."

Trying to avoid her probing gaze, he escorted her towards the refreshments area. "I gather you don't much approve of Castleberry." She probably went in for low Elizabethan halls in solid mahogany wainscoting with stuffed grouse everywhere. Steeplechasing in autumn and skiing at Gstaad over the Christmas holidays.

"It looks suspiciously like a Las Vegas casino knocked down and shipped here piece by piece," she acidly observed. "Ah well, at least here we won't have to put a coin in a slot for a drink."

Max scarcely heard her; he was distracted by the largest emerald he had ever seen, suspended against the white throat of an ethereally thin woman in a Dior batwing gown. He instantly knew who she was: the blue-blooded wife of Tony Hoggwell, the famous diet-book doctor.

"Do you like emeralds, Raffles?" his companion inquired.

"I adore them. And call me Max."

"Just call me Julia."

He met her smirk with an appreciative one of his own, as he turned and nodded at the Jacobite waiter behind the punchbowl. Max accepted two diamond-faceted goblets of pale pink punch from the waiter and handed one to Julia. They walked away from the relative crush at the drinks table and lounged next to a fountain choked with water lilies and stone nymphs taking a wee. Her eyes peered up at him over her drink. The large, brown, curious eyes of a tomboy grown up.

"Now, mysterious Max, what are you up to? As your ticket in, I deserve at least a good lie."

He gave her his best direct look. "Any particular sort of lie you'd fancy?"

"The more outlandish the better."

"I'm an undercover agent for the Inland Revenue. Dame Gwenna's been cheating on her taxes." They both laughed. He sipped at his drink and made a face. "Baby's bathwater." He downed it quickly, like medicine, and said, "Did you know, Julia, that little girls tend to build long, low walls out of toy blocks, while boys build high, shaky towers?"

She blinked. "Now you sound like a self-help bestseller."

He looked at her in surprise—it was one of his better party lines. "I'm working on a new tower tonight. Be a love and don't shake it down."

"You may rely on me," she assured him, putting an arm through his and adding, "Let's circulate."

He was about to try again with more chat, but they were both diverted by the sight of the unmistakably robust figure of their hostess, in full regalia, sweeping across the room like a queen. At least kitted out like one: the low-cut expanse of turquoise water-marked silk was pinched mercilessly about her generous curves. Lights glittered from bejeweled fingers, neck, ears, and haloed her mass of apricot-tinted curls. She was truly an impressive sight as she cruised along, her bow wave pushing aside minor sycophants, trailing a secretarial type behind her like a dinghy.

Gwenna Hardcastle came to a stop very close by and took the arm of a balding gentleman in horn rims. Pink lacquered nails sank into his arm as she said in an agitated voice that carried to Max and Julia: "Oh, Tony, it's like a nightmare! Now it's my ostrich-feather peignoir—deliberately *ruined*." Max was surprised at the hysterical edge to her voice. It was at odds with the public persona of the awesome upper-class writer of romances, the dominant figure of the London social pages for over four decades.

Max recognised Horn Rims from his dust jacket: Dr. Tony Hoggwell, in the flesh. He was a tanned, soft-faced man with a chipper manner. "Now, Gwenna, I shan't listen to wild talk of plots—especially not in public." Hoggwell cast a baleful eye at the press of fascinated onlookers, including a couple of high government ministers. Max thought it interesting that the doctor mentioned plots. The lady had said no such thing. ". . . and I advise you to get a grip on yourself."

With visible effort she regained self-control, replacing hysteria with venom. "Just wait until I discover who's behind this malicious trickery!"

"That's the stuff!" The doctor nodded approvingly, but Dame Gwenna had already swirled away into the crowd. Hoggwell took a stiff drink and muttered to himself. He and Max exchanged glances as Max and Julia strolled past. "The diet doctor," he whispered to Julia, but she didn't seem to care.

Nearby, shrieks of ersatz distress emanated from a dowdy woman dressed in what looked like one of Queen Elizabeth's old party dresses. She was pawing at her bosom as a fox-faced young man with longish blond hair dropped a cocktail prawn down her front and then proceeded to go after it. His cronies yelled, "Ten points to Freddie" and "Run it to ground!" The woman writhed in an excess of embarrassed sexiness as Freddie retrieved the morsel to local applause. Adjacent elders looked shocked or bored to varying degrees. Max got the impression that this was an old party trick of the lad's. Would a striptease with lampshade be next? With a cry of triumph Freddie dropped the shrimp into his mouth, then feigned an attack, spinning around as if looking for a place to be sick, zoning in with nasty inspiration on Julia's upper regions.

Max's long arm reached out and with no apparent effort stopped Freddie dead in his tracks. A zone of silence instantly fell on the immediate area as Freddie's face contorted with rage. Max flexed his muscles slightly; both he and Freddie were aware that the younger man's toes were clear of the floor. "Be a good lad, go throw buns at your pals," Max said genially.

"He doesn't know who Freddie is!" someone gasped.

"But he will," Freddie hissed as he fell from Max's grasp. He jostled through the crowd of friends, straightening his jacket as he glared back over his shoulder.

Julia treated Max with amusement slightly tinged with derision. "My big, strong man. May I feel your muscles?"

Max stiffened, feeling his cool evaporating in front of this extremely irritating young woman. But he managed to grin and mumble, "Me Lord Greystoke."

"I wonder." She gave him a long look that almost cracked his patent leather shoes. "Or the Sloane Ranger, perhaps?"

"I beg your pardon," someone said from behind them. They turned to see Dr. Hoggwell's reassuring smile. "After that little palaver with our dear Freddie, I'd like to stand you a drink. Before you're turfed out, that is." His expression was chummy.

"I take it Freddie owns the place." Max sighed resignedly. He was beginning to regret his stupid overreaction. Julia would have probably had no trouble protecting herself from shrimps—fresh or half-pickled. And it had jeopardised his game. "Frankly, I could use a drink. I'm Max Genader, by the way."

"And I'm Tony Hoggwell."

Max wrung his hand. "A pleasure to meet you, Doctor. Congratulations on the success of your book. And you've just opened another diet and health clinic in France somewhere, haven't you?"

The doctor bobbed his head. "In Marseilles. Come with me if you're a man who appreciates an excellent Scotch. And will you, Miss . . . ?"

"Carlisle. Julia Carlisle. That sounds like a fine idea."

He led them along one colonnaded wall and into the billiard room, which was unoccupied.

"Ah, leather and cheroots," Max grinned as he breathed in the masculine odor of Old Money.

The doctor unlatched a highboy and pulled out a squat bottle. "Glen Fiddich?" he asked Max, who devoutly replied he'd take it over those heathen blends any day. Tony Hoggwell agreed and poured two glasses. "And you, Miss Carlisle?"

"I'll have the same."

"A pleasure to pour Scotch for a lady. No one else in this matriarchy drinks much of the stuff." He gave her a glass, then restlessly perched on the edge of the snooker table. The cone-shaped pool of light from overhead made his pale eyes disappear behind the shadow of his spectacles. They sipped quietly for a moment, the sounds of the distant party filtering through the closed door.

Max broke their silence. "I take it something comes with the drink. A lecture on the house rules? You seem to know your way around."

"I'm here often enough. And I *would* like to address your admirable behaviour to one obnoxious young ass. Your health!" The doctor raised his glass, nothing but amiability in his manner. "The fellow you rather casually mishandled is the much-cosseted nephew of our hostess. Freddie's no prize at the best of times, and when he's had a few . . . well, to be charitable, he could win a spitting contest with a cobra. Not that he's what you might call a powerful specimen, but Gwenna dotes on him. And *she* certainly is a force to be reckoned with."

"So I've crossed swords with the little lord of the manor."

"Over a lady's honour," Julia added.

"And a pleasant sight it was! But I can only assume that you are mad, or you didn't know who Freddie was."

"Or don't care," Max shrugged.

"In Gwenna's house you had better care," the doctor declared. "Your lack of the properly cautious attitude must mean that you are strangers to this household."

"A shrewd guess," said Julia, earning herself a dark look from Max.

Hoggwell looked gratified. "I thought so. Gwenna has been ranting all evening about uninvited guests, so I did a little snooping and discovered that her so-called gate crashers were very much invited. Seems the guest list has been fiddled." He allowed himself a chuckle. "Am I correct that neither of you expected to receive your invitation?"

"It was a bit of a shock." Julia smiled sweetly at Max's studiously blank face.

"So I thought. Well, if anyone should ask, you are my personal guests. That's all I really wanted to say. Gwenna's parties are the same old stilted operas. Any new blood is more than welcome." He had the perfect professional smile that said everything was going to be all right, he would see to it.

"May I ask just what your connexion is to the Hardcastles—if you don't much like them?" Max wanted to know.

"My wife, Benecia, is Gwenna's cousin. I'm also Gwenna's personal physician and lately a partner in a business venture. Have you heard about Raptureland?" He could see from their expressions that they hadn't. "Well, I'll let you in on a little secret. Tonight Gwenna is planning a surprise announcement." He glanced at his watch. "Right about now."

"What is Raptureland?" Julia giggled. "I've always disliked the word *rapture* myself, reminds me of rupture."

"You too? I thought it was just my medical mind. I call it Raptureland behind her back. Officially, I am a one-third partner in the Gwenna Hardcastle Museum of Historical Romance. A concrete visualisation of her eighty-six novels. The Madame Tussaud's of love, you might say." Outside the music had stopped and the sound of a gong rang out. "That would be the announcement. Shall we?" Hoggwell held the door open for them.

Under a spotlight aimed down from a balcony, a Shakespearian fop was hamming it up on the steps of the stage. Beneath the long wig was the chinless wonder himself, Freddie Hardcastle. He was making a hash of proclaiming the official christening of the museum, but his aunt beamed approval by his side. Polite applause greeted what had obviously not been a well-kept secret.

"Now let's get the stockholders up here!" Freddie barked like a game-show host. "Doctor Hoggwell!" His smile faded as he noticed the doctor's companions. "Come up here, please, and bring that delicious slip of a wife—if you can find her!" The doctor lost his amiable expression.

"Once more into the breach," Hoggwell murmured. "Best of luck to you both," he said as he pushed off through the crowd.

"That crack about his wife didn't go down well," Julia remarked to Max.

"Not quite," he agreed, enjoying the undercurrents. The evening promised to be anything but dull.

A deep voice from nearby sarcastically muttered, "Let's hope Freddie doesn't call Sam Gary up on stage next."

Another voice knowingly replied that it wasn't likely. Gentlemen like Sam Gary had to stay out of the limelight, for business reasons.

"I'd like to know how that slimy little hood got to be a partner in the Hardcastle museum," a third chimed in.

Max looked around, glanced at the source of the last remark, then at Julia. "That's a fair question. From what I've heard, Sam Gary's a little out of place in this crowd."

"You should know." Julia's whisper was decidedly ironic. Her tone rankled. Max was having second thoughts about the lady; she wasn't making it any easier on him.

Benecia Hoggwell had just stepped up on stage and was squirming away from Freddie's show biz kiss. Max raised an eyebrow, but kept his eyes on the show. Freddie was now turning over the floor to his aunt. As the ovation filled the hall, Max looked speculatively at Julia and put his lips to her ear to be heard over the commotion. "Exactly where do *you* fit in, darling? I thought you must have been joking for my benefit when you told Hoggwell your invitation came as a shock."

"I haven't a clue why I was invited. I don't mingle with the peerage, as a rule," she answered after the noise had subsided. Max was too stunned to reply. Just a few feet away Freddie made his way past, muttering, "My codpiece is killing me."

Unaware of her sudden fall from grace, Julia grinned at Freddie's absurd getup. "Life of the party, our Freddie."

Meanwhile Gwenna was promising everyone a dramatic treat within the hour, her voice slurring just perceptibly. Oblivious to the oohhs and aahhs of anticipation, Max frowned at Julia. "But you looked so right!" he insisted.

"Sorry, I'm non-U through and through. Common as dirt." She didn't even seem to give a damn.

"Go on, pull the other one."

She could only laugh in disbelief at this peculiar new turn their conversation had taken. "Come on!" she cried. "You're twitching your nose as if I'd just confessed to a penchant for cannibalism!"

Without a word Max turned on his heel and evaporated into the mob, leaving Julia staring open-mouthed after him. By the time she had recovered and made up her mind to go after him, he was lost in a sea of dinner-jacketed males. Circling the dance floor in an effort to spot him, she accepted a drink from a servant's tray and downed it in three gulps. The alcohol enhanced the surrealistic detachment overtaking her. She found herself focusing on chins sagging and bobbing comically as party babble gushed forth in relentless gobbles.

Wearying of it all and considering the advantages of a timely exit, Julia took momentary refuge in the powder room. It was a modest little lounge, fitted out in flocked lavender wallpaper and gold cupids spitting hot and cold. A boyish figure was bent over one of the sculpted marble basins, splashing water on her brow. Julia was vaguely aware of a faint, acrid smell underneath the artificial bouquet of air freshener.

The woman gave a start as she caught sight of Julia in the mirror. "Oh! I didn't hear you come in," Benecia Hoggwell said. She was a perfect advertisement for her husband's diet book.

"Are you ill?" Julia inquired.

"I'm fine now. Silly of me to drink so much." She gestured obscurely towards the sink. "Dangerous on an empty stomach."

"I have some mints, if you'd like."

Mrs. Hoggwell shook her head, scooping up her purse and turning to face Julia directly. "You're marvelously thin," she breathed, stroking Julia's arm with clammy fingers, before abruptly going out the door.

Twirling a lock of hair, Julia stared at her own reflection and said, "What a ghastly party." Her charming escort's sudden, inexplicable desertion. The friendly, confidential doctor with his Trilby of a wife. The terrible Gwenna, her foul nephew. Even the band was depressing. The silent cupids winked sweetly up at her. She sighed as she quit their easy companionship. Once more into the fray; the things one did for detective aunties.

She returned to the ballroom to the dying echoes of a trumpet fanfare. The lights had been dimmed and

Gwenna Hardcastle was again in the spotlight, motioning for someone to join her from the crowd. A tall man with a wild head of white hair joined Gwenna on stage and blinked out at the audience. He had slightly stooped shoulders and a seedy professorial air about him. He grimaced as the photographer snapped away.

"No museum can be great without great art," Gwenna declared, holding a dramatic pose for the camera. "And here is our wonderfully gifted artist, Leonard Cheevers." The ovation swelled and Gwenna held up her hands for silence. "In my writing I've always hoped to capture the great moments of human passion played across the momentous events in history. Hearts that have lived and loved brilliantly across the centuries still live today!" Gwenna paused for another round of applause. Julia thought the speech sounded like the dreck off the back of a Hardcastle paperback. And that Hardcastle looked as though she'd had a bit too much of the baby's bathwater to drink.

"Bacon!" Gwenna suddenly shouted, awkwardly stepping down from the stage, the artist right behind her. "The lights, please!" Shutters clattered up on the balcony as the butler dimmed the spotlamp. The house lights went out, leaving the room in total darkness. Someone coughed. Then the distinct creak of wheels could be heard as something large was rolled into the ballroom from the hall at the foot of the stairs. It squeaked slowly towards them. Julia thought she heard a door click closed farther away.

"Ladies and gentlemen," their hostess stage-whispered into the hush, making the most of the moment. "May I present our Greatest Writer and his fabulous Dark Lady!" Her voice rose at the end; on cue the spotlamp snapped on, illuminating a startlingly realistic balcony scene, complete with rose trellis and open mullioned windows above. Centered in the circle of light was a beautiful woman, her Elizabethan décolletage leaning over the railing as she gazed down into the dark. The guests gasped at the astonishing accuracy of the figure, scarcely distinguishable from a living person.

Gwenna gave the word and her unseen butler panned the spotlamp downwards, lighting up the rest of the diorama. It was a visualisation of the balcony scene from *Romeo and Juliet*—but the earthbound supplicant, standing with one knee bent, was none other than William Shakespeare.

More flashbulbs exploded. There were appreciative responses from the audience, gasps, chuckles, scattered applause as people reacted to the details of the scene. Julia's eye was quick to settle on the unexpected element. There was a third figure on the stage of the tableau, a costumed man flat on his back to one side of Shakespeare's figure. Compositionally it was decidedly comic, the bearded writer gazing up at his lady love, a dead chevalier rejected at his feet—a neat comment on the Bard's alleged sexual ambivalence. Shakespeare's scabbard was empty, the épée neatly skewering the victim through the heart. There was even some authentic-looking blood. Julia swayed on her feet, mumbling an appropriate line from the Bard: "Slipped cold steel twixt his gizzard and his gut." She suddenly felt very sick.

"Look! One of the statues is Freddie!" someone hooted.

"The ham!"

"You can blink now, Freddie!"

A woman screamed at the front of the crowd. Gwenna Hardcastle, her voice shrill with horror, cried out, "Freddie! Oh my God!" Julia's sick suspicion had been correct. Someone had given a new meaning to the word diorama.

Even though she instantly knew what she should do, Julia hesitated, half-expecting Freddie to leap to his feet covered in fake blood. But Doctor Hoggwell, the first to climb up onto the set, dropped Freddie's limp wrist and shook his head. The rest of the lights came on, revealing Gwenna staring bug-eyed into the tableau. There was an ugly red splash of blood on the front of her turquoise silk skirt.

In the ensuing confusion it was easy for Julia to detach herself and make her way towards the hall, the only way they could have brought the diorama into the ballroom. The door was still open, an overhead light now on as an anxious servant stood by, uncertain of what was happening.

"You're needed!" Julia told him, letting a note of panic steal into her voice. "There's been a terrible accident!" The servant hesitated, then hastily closed the swinging double doors behind him and dashed towards the commotion.

Julia slipped through the swinging doors into what apparently were the private quarters. Thick purple carpet absorbed the sounds of chaos from the ballroom. Clearly visible in the deep pile were the wheel marks left by the diorama. A few cautious steps brought her to a junction of two passageways; one led to the left and up a flight of stairs, the other straight towards a pair of French doors at the end. She moved quietly straight on and peered out the French doors into the dark garden. The doors had only inside handles.

She turned round and retraced her steps, pausing uneasily in front of another door. The wheel tracks on the rug indicated that something heavy had been wheeled in from outside, into this room, then transported down the hall to the ballroom. She was afraid to try the door, for fear of meeting the murderer inside. And what if it were Max? His gate-crashing and adroit evasions had taken on a sinister flavour. That brief tussle with Freddie—had there been a second and final round? And what about that object she'd felt in his breast pocket while they were dancing? A gun?

She carefully turned down the gold latch with the hem of her skirt; this was no time to smudge fingerprints. The door swung open. She took a deep breath and flicked a light switch, and found herself in an unoccupied room that apparently served as a library. The carpet was rolled up to one side, exposing a generous expanse of oak parquet. The furniture had been pushed together against one wall, presumably to make more floor space. She stooped down and looked at dull streaks in the wax. The diorama must have been stored here before the showing. As she was straightening up, a bit of dirt on the floor caught her eye. She picked it up. It looked like straw and smelled of horse manure.

She paced around, trying to memorise every detail. Below the shelves of morocco-bound volumes stood a pink-marble-topped Regency table with gilt trim. Crammed beside it were several easy chairs and black-shaded brass reading lamps. Noticing nothing out of the ordinary, she turned her attention to a second door beside the fireplace.

No one was inside this adjoining room either, which turned out to be a private study with a fire burning in the dramatic marble fireplace. It was furnished with a chaise and matching love seat in apricot chintz, but the room was dominated by a black japanned writing desk and bookcase, every inch of its surface shimmering with Oriental scenes. There was a plain wooden filing cabinet in one corner, its top packed with flattering photographs of Gwenna from infancy to age forty. The only other furniture was a small liquor cabinet, the bevelled glass door not quite closed. An empty Waterford decanter sat on the desk next to a matching soda siphon; there was also a highball glass with a small amount of amber liquid in the bottom.

Julia knelt and sniffed the glass, detecting the unmistakable scent of Scotch. She found a stain on the rug beside the desk that also smelled like Scotch. There was another, smaller stain nearby that seemed to be blood.

She got to her feet and examined the contents of the liquor cabinet. Six crystal glasses on one shelf with space for two more. One was on the desk. The other one appeared to be missing.

How did it all fit together? Spilled Scotch, a little blood, a missing glass, Freddie skewered at Shakespeare's feet. Several times during the evening she had noticed the footman at his post in front of the private hallway. She tried to recall if he had been there all evening. It seemed so. If he had, it was doubtful that anyone could have gotten to this part of the house without being observed.

She had left the study and was crossing the library, determined to have a look round the garden, when a muffled moan stopped her in her tracks. Her gaze swept the room. Nothing had apparently changed, and the door to the hall remained closed. She tiptoed across to the rolled-up carpet and tested it with her toe, working her way down until a lump resisted her weight. When she stepped down harder, the lump groaned again.

A tug at the flap of the carpet exposed a dinner-jacketed form. Blood matted down the hair on the side of his head. Even before rolling him over, Julia was certain it was Max. He was unconscious and breathing stentoriously, obviously in need of medical attention. But she found herself calmly deciding that there were some things she had better know about him right now, if only for her own protection. After all, as the woman who had gotten him through the front door, she was involved.

She quickly went through his pockets, removing his house key and wallet. She noted the address on his ID, then frowned over his business card before slipping it and the key into her purse. The other significant find was in his breast pocket. He'd been telling the truth—it *was* one of those miniaturized cameras carried by the cinema variety of spy. Apparently by other kinds as well. She pocketed the camera, grimacing at the thought of how the police would interpret such brazen fiddling of the evidence.

She studied his pale face for a moment. Without his lively, smiling mask he looked less handsome and more vulnerable. Tracing the strong line of his jaw to his square, dimpled chin, she wondered who this man really was. A dashing burglar? A magazine reporter? Or the Max Genader on his business card—seller of fine, previously owned motorcars.

It was a small but tastefully furnished flat overlooking Hampstead Heath. Julia quelled an impulse to take a quick look and get out fast. It wasn't nice to go through a stranger's personal effects, but it had to be done. Self-preservation and her amateur detective's instincts demanded it.

There was a pile of car magazines beside the bed, another in the bathroom, yet a third by an Italian chrome-and-leather chair in the living room. There was a closetful of very good quality clothes. A maroon velours bathrobe was dropped on the bathroom tile, but the sink was spotless. No hairs in the tub, either. There were too many bottles of wildly masculine cologne on the vanity, and a pinky signet ring and pair of diamond cuff links shaped like steering wheels. She ran her hand over the surface of the night table. No dust, just some spilled talc.

Finally she sat down at the desk and went through his papers. There was a box of business cards for Max Genader, Gosport Motorcars Ltd. Jaguar, Rolls-Royce, Lamborghini, and Other Fine Motorcars. A bundle of letters from his sister in America was full of chatty news of two kids, a husband, and life in New York. The bottom drawer was crammed with receipts for paid bills. He spent a lot of money on clothes, dined out, and did a fair amount of foreign travelling, according to his credit card vouchers. A suite in Cannes, frequent visits to a hotel in Monte Carlo, several expensive dinners in Paris, a three-piece suit recently purchased in Milano. For a car salesman, he got around.

But she discovered the real key to Max's character in the bookcase, right next to the Dick Francis novels. Masquerading as an ordinary-looking scrapbook, it turned out to be an extraordinary record of an odd passion. Mementos of smart parties, photos clipped out of tabloids of important social events, all showing Max in an exclusive crowd of celebrants. Shots of familiar faces putting on the feed bag. Max walking behind Princess Margaret at Wimbledon. Max on a yacht only a few bodies away from rubbing shoulders with Jackie O. Underneath the photos were neat, printed comments on the event: the people who were there, who he sat beside at dinner, what famous personality he got to chat up. It was a chronicle of total fascination with the upper classes—especially upper-class women. In a cruise shot Max stood grinning at a gorgeous blonde in a tiny bikini. The same woman in silk shirt and jeans smiled out from behind a frame on the coffee table. "All my love, Mary Anne." According to Max's notes, first cousin to the Duke of Basingstoke and very jet set. Her sister had married a Rothschild. There was a photo of Max and Mary Anne at the wedding; they made a handsome couple.

Feeling like a voyeur, Julia closed the album. Apparently he was just a car salesman with a weakness for crashing society parties. It seemed preposterous enough to be true, and explained why he dropped her. She was just the wrong sort. Reasonable behaviour for a social-climbing smoothie with no time for a little nobody like herself.

She went into the kitchen and looked in his fridge. One can learn a lot about a person by what's on the shelf. There was a bottle of ale, a frozen pizza, a huge jar of cocktail onions and a split of very nice champagne, two eggs, and a matching number of sausages. The ale and sausage might indicate working-class origins. The frozen pizza, a rare find in London, hinted that he'd developed an appetite for American fast food—visiting his sister, perhaps. The champagne was no doubt chilling for the next time Mary Anne dropped by.

2

PHYLLIS HATED HOOVERING more than anything. She would rather wash windows or get down on her knees and scrub floors. But dogs made it necessary to vacuum at least once a week. They shed hair and tracked in mud. They chewed up slippers and left bits of them behind the sofa. If it wasn't for that bloody terrier, her job would be a snap. Such were Phyllis's thoughts as she dragged the nozzle back and forth across the rug, giving Tim a nudge with the point of her shoe when he got in the way, which was often. He liked to grab the hose of the cleaner, intent on biting holes in the long neck of the invader. The roaring monster must be driven off Tim's own turf. Such were the terrier's thoughts as he darted between Phyllis's legs, causing her to trip over the cord, pulling the plug from the wall socket. There was a sudden silence, followed by a terrible explosion behind her.

She clutched her heart and sank to her knees, twisting round in the direction of the bang. Terror was instantly replaced by fury, then by a kind of triumph as the cleaning woman stared up at the revolver in her employer's tiny hand.

"You're trying to kill me! It's finally happened like I always knew it would!" Phyllis shouted, ducking behind the couch. "All that murder you write about has finally driven you mad!"

"Nonsense, I was only firing blanks to discover if someone would hear the report of a revolver over the din of a vacuum cleaner," Lettie Winterbottom cheerfully explained, tucking a pin back into her silvery curls. "The machine's noise renders the operator as good as deaf, an ineffective witness to, say, a shooting committed upstairs."

"A likely story!" Phyllis sniffed. "You were going to shoot me, and I know it. This is the last straw. I quit." With that declaration, the cleaning lady stood up and marched out of the house, leaving Lettie wringing her hands and muttering. Domestic help in St. Martin's Mere was difficult to come by. Nobody wanted to clean his own house, let alone someone else's.

"What will I do?" Lettie moaned. She was getting too old to be shoving a heavy cleaner around. The doctor had even ordered her to find someone to help with the garden, since she'd been having this trouble with her back. But Lettie was stubborn. She grabbed the cleaner and started dragging it resolutely across the carpet. A person just had to soldier on, arthritis be damned. But she winced as she replaced the plug in the socket.

The noise of the machine prevented her from hearing Tim yapping excitedly at her niece, Julia, who first tapped at the window, rang the bell, then finally opened the door and stepped inside. As a result it made Lettie's heart leap when she turned around and found someone standing on her living room rug. She kicked the button with her foot and the racket died.

"Julia! You gave me such a start!"

"Sorry, Auntie. What are you doing with that cleaner? You know it's bad for your back," Julia scolded, all the while trying to rescue the sleeve of her grey suede jacket from the jaws of the terrier welcoming committee.

Lettie sighed and said, "Phyllis quit."

"What now?"

"She thinks I'm trying to kill her."

"Ridiculous!" Julia giggled and almost added, "But typical."

"Isn't it? The woman's paranoid . . . I suppose it was the revolver that did it."

"The revolver?"

"Yes, my brother's old service revolver. Full of blanks, of course. An experiment required before I could get down to writing chapter seven of *Murder by Tabby*."

"The killer uses a cat?"

"Mmm-hmm. The handsome victim is suffocated with a docile tabby while he sleeps."

"While the cat sleeps? What's the victim doing?"

"No, no, while the victim sleeps. And the second murder is even bolder. A revolver fired upstairs while the maid is vacuuming downstairs. The noise of the cleaner prevents the maid from hearing the shot. It really would—I just verified it on Phyllis."

Julia rolled her eyes. "I'm beginning to get the picture. How are you going to get her back?"

"What if I offered her ten more pounds a month?" Lettie suggested doubtfully, hanging her head. Phyllis had her over a barrel.

"That might not do it this time."

"Would you talk to her, dear? She seems to . . ."

"All right, Auntie."

"Thank you. Now, tell me all about the party."

"Why should I? You stood me up," the younger woman teased.

Lettie looked shamefaced. "I'm sorry. My nerve failed me at the last minute. I just couldn't fathom getting an invitation from *her*. I looked for pictures in this morning's paper, but there was nothing. Did I miss much?"

"Just the same old stuff," came Julia's deadpan reply.

"A handsome, mysterious gate-crasher, watery punch, and a murder."

Lettie caught her breath, her blue eyes widening as she cried, "You're joking!"

"I wish I were."

"Oh my! Sit down! Tell me everything!" Lettie dithered until they were settled in chairs before the window overlooking the garden. "Who is this handsome gate-crasher?"

"His name is Max Genader. Seems to be nothing more sinister than a used-car salesman and society groupie. But the police aren't going to like him much. He quarreled with Freddie Hardcastle—the victim—in front of several witnesses."

"What did they quarrel about?"

"Me."

"As I live and breathe!" Lettie exclaimed, her cheeks turning pink with excitement. "Start at the beginning."

Julia obediently outlined the scene of the crime as she remembered it. The blood on the carpet seemed to indicate that Freddie was killed in the study, although there was also a big pool of blood on the floor of the diorama itself. Barring secret passages, there were only three means of access to the murder room: the locked French doors leading outside at one end of the hall, the swinging doors guarded by a servant at the other end, and the stairs.

Julia described the diorama, the library and study, then launched into the fascinating subject of Max, his peculiar hobby, his charm, and her sudden abandonment when he learned she was a nobody. Rudeness aside, how had he gotten past the guard and into the murder room? What was he doing in there? "He makes an excellent suspect if you can explain how he committed the murder, then rolled up in the rug and knocked himself unconscious."

"Simple," Lettie replied. "Someone walked in after he'd killed Freddie. There was a struggle, Max was rendered . . ."

"Then why roll him up in the rug?"

Lettie mulled it over before suggesting, "To make him appear innocent. The work of an accomplice."

Julia looked dubious. "I can't imagine Max killing someone. He didn't even know Freddie."

"Perhaps not. But he still might have reason for wanting him dead."

"It just doesn't feel right," Julia insisted.

"Can he really be just a car salesman with an odd hobby?"

"Well, he has a good salesman's smoothness. And there are car magazines all over his apartment."

"His apartment?" Lettie's eyebrows arched towards her widow's peak.

"I stole his key. His camera, too."

Lettie blinked in amazement at the dear girl's casual confession. "He was carrying a camera?"

"Mm-hmm. To take photos of celebrities for his collection. I thought he might have snapped something pertinent, so I nicked it off him before anybody else got the chance."

"Tsk tsk! The police won't take this very . . ."

"Kindly?" Julia habitually finished any sentences her aunt left dangling. "Probably not. But we'll get to see what's on the film as soon as it comes back from the chemist."

"That will be lovely."

They next discussed the Hardcastle ménage—Freddie's kissing up to his aunt, and his generally caddish behaviour towards females. "I'd venture that there were any number of women at the party who would have had good reason to run him through."

"Revenge is such a nice motive, so Greek," Lettie sighed. "But one can't use it in every book."

Lettie was most fascinated by Julia's description of Dame Gwenna (whom Lettie had never met but long disliked) and the rumours of a mental breakdown. Was someone truly playing tricks on her, or was she just imagining it? Could she be that paranoid? And how could uninvited guests show up with bona fide invitations? "At least we have the explanation for one little mystery," Lettie remarked. "We now know why she invited me—she didn't. Somebody else did in order to annoy La Grande Dame." She smiled grimly, gratified by the implications.

To Lettie's mind, Gwenna Hardcastle had always been a bane to good writers everywhere. Hardcastle wrote the most awful romance novels, particularly galling as they always sold millions of copies. To add insult to injury, the old snob flaunted her success, forever looking down her nose at reporters and saying how tiresome it was to have to give interviews to the sort she wouldn't even have talked to if it were still the nineteenth century.

Lettie whitened when she heard about the plans for the museum. This was beyond the pale—opening a museum to oneself! She gritted her teeth and furiously brushed at the dog hair on her chair. Eventually Lettie regained her temper enough to request calmly the details of how the diorama was brought in, saying that putting the body in the diorama was very significant. After all, if the killer had known the diorama was to be displayed, leaving the body there assured maximum shock value. On the other hand, the murderer might have thought the diorama was a good place to hide his victim, if he hadn't expected the whole scene to come under such immediate public scrutiny.

"But why hide it there instead of under a shrub in the garden?"

"And risk carrying a bleeding body down the hall to get out the French doors?"

"Good point!" Julia conceded. "Speaking of blood—there was some on Gwenna's skirt."

"That's rather awkward, isn't it? Might she have killed him, if he'd gotten her angry enough?"

"Judging from what I saw of him, he could make anybody angry enough. But if his aunt killed him she surely would have foregone showing the diorama, knowing we were bound to notice it."

"But it wouldn't have been wise for her to change her plans. You said several people knew she intended to show it. Wouldn't it have looked suspicious if she had changed her mind?"

"And if she's innocent, how did the blood get on her skirt?"

Lettie clasped her hands together and closed her eyes. "Suppose . . . suppose she went into the library to check the diorama, brushed against the front of it, and got blood on her skirt that way."

"If she did that she would have noticed Freddie's corpse!"

"Of course. Very well, she went into the library for another reason, barely looking at the diorama as she brushed past . . ." Lettie was more than a little bemused, chasing permutations like Tim after his own tail.

"A clandestine meeting?" Julia ventured.

"I like that. Clandestine meetings are the very backbone of plot."

The two women had been discussing the case for over an hour when the phone rang. Lettie picked up the receiver and found herself listening to the halting preamble from a Mrs. Janet Batney, who identified herself as Gwenna Hardcastle's secretary. Lettie gasped and excitedly waved her niece over to the phone, holding the instrument away from her ear so they both could listen.

". . . So glad you were there and witnessed the . . . horror with your own eyes. I mean, because you're such a keen observer!" The poor secretary backtracked valiantly.

"But I didn't accept the invitation," Lettie politely explained. "However, my niece attended and just informed me of the tragedy. I was very sorry to hear of it."

"Then you'll come to my employer's aid? She requested that I call and stress how much you're needed here."

"I find that fascinating, since Dame Gwenna and I have never met."

"An acquaintance told her about your reputation for discreet investigation."

"I'm flattered."

"She needs help, Miss Winterbottom. Her nerves are shattered, and she can't tolerate talking to the police again. They treat her like a suspect, making an already dreadful situation unbearable."

"I quite understand. It must have come as a nasty shock. Please convey my condolences to your employer."

"I shall. And when may we expect you?"

"Please don't expect me. I doubt very much that I could do more than the police."

"Oh, please don't refuse, Miss Winterbottom! The mistress has her mind made up. She thinks the Force is against her."

"You may assure your employer that if she is innocent, she has nothing to fear from the police, Mrs. Batney." Lettie used kindly tones, which somewhat softened the implication of her words. Julia made a face and waved her hands, but Lettie shook her head. "Good-bye, Mrs. Batney. I am so sorry I can't be of further help." Lettie hung up with a little smile, the closest thing to nastiness that Julia had ever seen on her aunt's normally angelic features.

"Auntie! I'll never understand you!" Julia groaned.

"Why not?"

"How could you pass up such an opportunity?"

"What? To humbly serve the great Hardcastle?"

"No, no—the case! Aren't you itching to poke your nose in?"

"Of course, but one learns self-control. Besides, one should never sell oneself cheap, especially when coming to the aid of the despicable."

For a few moments the only sound was the next-door neighbour raking the leaves off the sidewalk, the mantel clock ticking, and Tim licking the kitchen floor. Julia chewed her lip and tried to control her frustration.

"But, Auntie—"

The phone rang again. "Ah!" Lettie smugly beamed. "That will be the great Hardcastle herself, or I'll eat my bridgework!"

3

A RECENT PSYCHOLOGICAL STUDY HAS determined that most men find photographs of nudes sexually stimulating, while most women do not. Given their druthers, nine out of ten women will purchase a romantic novel over a photograph of a nude male lounging against a pool table anyday. Real men don't read romantic novels over their quiche, which is probably just as well. If men read Hardcastle novels they would probably get the erroneous impression that nothing appeals to a woman more than the likelihood of being raped. On horseback, if possible. Her heroines were eternally fighting off lusty lords astride huge black stallions. The expanses of velvet bodice torn from snowy, heaving bosoms in these stories would be enough to recurtain the Albert Hall. And such encounters always left the owners of the snowy bosoms annoyed but fascinated in spite of themselves. This pretty much covered Hardcastle's deep understanding of the female psyche.

Coming from a long line of Hardcastle stableboys, Hal Skinner at seventeen was a hopelessly weedy ruffian with blotchy skin and very little hair. He had delicate bone structure and a propensity for spitting. Grooming Hardcastle's horses was a good life until the night the white gelding took sick and lay down in his stall, pinning poor Hal underneath. Hal shouted for help, but no one heard him. The pain went away in a few hours, replaced by a terrible numbness and a panicky boredom. He knew full well that he might be stuck under this bloody animal all night. What was he to do in the meantime? A good night's sleep was definitely out.

His left arm and right leg were free, the rest of his body trapped beneath several hundredweight of ailing thoroughbred. He found that by stretching his leg he could slide it underneath the stall wall and out into the entryway. He experimented with this for a while, dragging his foot along, seeing what he could find. It was a thrill when his toe hit something. The next hour flew by as he tried to manoeuvre that something into the stall with him, all the while hoping for a sausage sandwich. But his hopes were dashed when he succeeded in bringing the object close enough to determine that it was a paperback novel. He edged it closer and discovered that it was a Hardcastle romance—*The Haughty Duchess and the Stableboy Prince,* to be exact.

Hal had never read a Hardcastle novel; in fact, he had never read any novel. It was a new experience that helped pass the remaining seven hours before he was discovered and rescued.

The experience left him with some broken ribs, a slight limp, and a damaged psyche. Being young, he recovered quickly from being pinned under a foundering horse all night; but he never did get over that novel. Under the pressure of horseflesh and pain he became convinced that he actually was the lost Scottish prince and Gwenna Hardcastle his destined mate. He went about his humble daily chores and brooded over this cruel twist of fate until it ate away at his very insides. What chance did he have to prove his noble blood as long as everyone still called him "Little Hal Skinner, prettier but not much brighter than the other Skinners"?

And how could he continue to live with his consuming passion for the haughty author of those love scenes that inflamed his desires? What hope of winning her when she was a cousin to the Royal Family and he was the dirt beneath her spike heels? To make matters worse, she had fifty years and sixty pounds on him, which might cause problems if he ever got a chance to pull her down into the hay and tear the velvet bodice from those magnificent alabaster mounds. (And him without even a riding crop he could call his own.)

Such were Hal's tortured thoughts as he hovered at the violent edge of despair. If only he could commit some outrageous act to get her attention. But what could he do? There were no wars to join. He toyed with the idea of setting fire to the house in order to rescue her from the flames of death, but he had no confidence in his own ability to pick her up and carry her.

"Hal!" his stable master would shout. "Quit yer damned day-dreamin' and muck out the stables!"

The torment went on for weeks until the miracle happened. He and the Object of his Desires established contact.

Lettie took a train to London, then a cab to the Hardcastle estate, which managed to look like a grand country manor in spite of the surrounding city. By the time the cabby dropped her off at the gigantic doors of Castleberry, she was quivering with nervous anticipation. She dreaded coming face-to-face with the Queen of Historical Romance at last and hoped to find the internal fortitude that the occasion would certainly require.

The door was opened by a fine figure of a butler in a morning coat that matched his perfect black hair. Bacon looked to be in his late forties, but the dyed hair might have hidden some telltale grey. He was the quintessential butler except for the eye patch. Eye patches were well and good on sailors, but never on butlers, Lettie thought as Bacon showed her into the Emerald Room, where Janet Batney was waiting.

"Oh, Miss Winterbottom!" the secretary cried in one of those faint voices that are inaudible three feet away. "You don't know how grateful we are to you for coming!" Mrs. Batney was a pear-shaped, middle-aged person in a navy skirt and starched white blouse. Her obvious nervousness dispelled some of Lettie's own.

"It must be difficult for all of you," Lettie murmured sympathetically.

"Just a bit," the secretary said bravely as she gave Lettie her pick of green brocaded chairs. The whole room was in shades of emerald with bamboo accents. It made Lettie feel slightly ill.

"I shall rely upon you to put me in the picture."

"I shall do my best. The mistress is rather a demanding person." Which probably explained Mrs. Batney's permanent smile that bordered on a grimace. Lettie imagined the poor creature even smiled in her sleep. "And she's been more difficult lately, with all the jokes—or should I say accidents? And now this horrible murder!"

"Start with the jokes."

"Dame Gwenna believes that someone is trying to drive her mad. And just between you and me . . ." She lowered her barely audible voice so that Lettie had to lean forward to catch her next words. "If it's true, they are succeeding! There have been late-night calls with only the baaing of sheep in the background."

"You mean no one speaks?" Lettie asked. The secretary shook her head. "How odd."

"Isn't it! Poor Bacon leaps out of bed and runs for

the phone, but the mistress has answered several of these calls before he could reach it."

"How many of these sheep calls have there been?"

"Six or seven in the past few months. Then a piece of furniture was moved and the mistress tripped over it and bruised her knee."

"Well, that doesn't sound like anything."

"I agree, these things do happen; but she thinks it's part of the harassment. Then her favourite peignoir came back ruined from the cleaners. And the caviar had to be discarded because it smelled like almonds. Sometimes the door bell gets stuck and has to be disconnected to keep it from ringing constantly. All little annoyances, but they do add up."

"I should think so!"

"Every time something happens, she goes to pieces and calls Dr. Hoggwell. She's become very dependent on him—quite a change . . . Of course, the party was a disaster from the beginning. Somebody tampered with the guest list. I'm afraid I'm the prime suspect." Mrs. Batney's smile tightened even more. "The mistress handed me a typed list that I put on my desk. I didn't have a chance to actually read it until the next day, when I sent out the invitations."

"So someone could have substituted another list?"

"It's the only explanation. There were the usual important names—royalty, politicians, leaders in science and industry with the right connexions. But there were a few odd ones: a punk rock singer, the shin-kicking champion from Lancashire, an Australian mountain climbing team."

"And myself."

"Oh no, I'm certain you were a valid guest!" the secretary insisted, blushing helplessly.

"It's all right, Mrs. Batney. I knew the invitation must

have been a mistake, and didn't accept. Please bring me the list."

The secretary quickly produced it, and they chuckled over the inclusion of several critics who had lambasted Hardcastle's novels, two rival writers besides Lettie, along with Hardcastle's former agent, to whom she hadn't spoken since 1957.

"Didn't you suspect this might be wrong?"

"I didn't recognise all of the names, of course, but I knew a couple were a bit off. I didn't think too much about it, though, since I knew she was going to announce the museum at the party. If there's one thing my employer enjoys, it's flaunting her triumphs in the envious faces of her critics."

"I hope you don't categorise me with that lot," Lettie said.

"Of course not!" The unfortunate woman had done it again. "You are a successful author in your own right."

"Oh, I'll never match the volume of Hardcastle sales."

"But you're just as famous—especially after finding Stonehenge and making them give it back. You were on the front page for weeks."

"Speaking of front page," Lettie said, "I understand there was a society photographer at the party."

"Yes, Norton Montegue from *The Sun*. I had to call him this morning and order him not to publish his pictures. He was very cooperative. The police had already told him to delay. They don't want anything in the papers for a few days."

"I'd like to see Mr. Montegue's photos." At that juncture of the conversation an awkward young woman burst into the room. "Janet, I need—" She trailed off when she saw Lettie and quickly gulped out an "Excuse me."

Mrs. Batney introduced her as Penny Smith, Hardcastle's young research assistant. Penny was a doughy-skinned redhead who hadn't yet discovered the wonders of mascara or the importance of good posture. She looked about twenty, slightly overweight, and very ill at ease.

"Miss Winterbottom is here to investigate the murder," Mrs. Batney explained. "We must tell her everything she wants to know."

Panic fluttered in Penny's green eyes, which would have been attractive if they'd had discernible lashes or brows around them. "I don't know anything. You know I'm never allowed to come to the parties," she said to Janet, avoiding Lettie's gaze.

"Were you in the house at the time?" Lettie inquired.

"I was upstairs in my room."

Lettie made a mental note to find out who else was upstairs.

"Penny lives here," Mrs. Batney explained. "The mistress likes to keep her close; she relies so completely on Penny's research."

"I'm sure you're invaluable," Lettie said and smiled at Penny, who mumbled that she'd better get back to work and left. "Is she always this shy?"

The secretary nodded. "She's at a difficult age. It would help if she could socialise. It isn't natural for a girl to have no friends."

"No indeed! Why doesn't she?"

"She is a little backward. But the mistress makes it worse by discouraging her from leaving the grounds."

Thinking she'd already had enough of "the mistress," Lettie asked why.

"Professional paranoia, you might call it. Penny researches historical detail and reports directly to Dame Gwenna. Romance is a rough business. The mistress lives in fear that someone will steal her ideas."

Lettie said that seemed a bit extreme. Fans would

buy her books whether there was a similar book written by another author or not.

Mrs. Batney agreed. "But the mistress takes secrecy to extremes. She will only write while locked up in her private study, which is just next to the library."

"Wasn't the diorama stored in the library?"

"That is correct. It was brought in just before seven o'clock last evening." There was silence for a moment, then the secretary shuddered. "The police found blood in the study; they believe Freddie was murdered in there! The mistress went to pieces when she heard about it. The study is her private refuge. It's kept locked and no one else is allowed in."

"Tell me more about her writing habits. As a fellow writer, I'm always interested in how others work."

"She writes a rough draft—which she won't let anyone see—then dictates from that draft to me."

"How many drafts does she do?"

"Just one."

"That explains a lot," Lettie muttered. "A lot of bad writing," she was tempted to add, but she bit it back.

"The police have been all over the house, of course. They keep asking about the mistress's movements during the party. It's the blood on her skirt; it looks very bad for her."

"Mmm. I understand there was a servant posted at the hall entrance?"

"Yes. Monte. For security reasons. There are a lot of valuable art pieces and antiques in the private wing."

"Is anything missing?"

The secretary shook her head, saying they'd inventoried it all very carefully. "The police talked to Monte quite a long time, wanting to know if he'd been at his post all evening, who'd been down the hall, that sort of thing. He told them no one but Freddie and Bacon—oh yes, and earlier on Cheevers, the artist, helped bring the diorama into the library. The police seem to think Monte is lying to protect his employer."

"Or his employment," Lettie guessed.

"Not Monte! He'd tell the truth, no matter what."

"And was he at his post all evening?"

"Yes, starting around seven, when the guests began arriving. He says he only left twice. Once, briefly, to answer the phone, which was just around the corner. The other servants were too busy at that moment to answer it."

"What time was that?"

"Around half past eight, shortly after Freddie announced the museum. Monte was only away for a few minutes. Just long enough to take a phone message for one of Freddie's friends."

"But was it long enough for someone to sneak down the hall?" When the secretary said it was possible, Lettie asked what time Monte was distracted for the second time.

"He says about ten minutes after that, when a gentleman called him over to mop up a spill."

"Any idea who that gentleman was?"

"I don't know his name, but he was the same one they found knocked out in the library."

The roses had returned to his cheeks, if not the twinkle to his eye. There was a thick bandage on the back of his head that spoiled the line of his perfect haircut. "And I can't find a nurse around here who can give me a manicure," he grumbled.

"The suffering must be intolerable!" Julia's voice exaggerated sympathy. "They say the danger of hangnail increases the longer you let your cuticles go."

"I'll make them give me more painkiller if it comes to that." He looked in very good spirits and as handsome as ever. When she handed him his keys and camera he seemed startled, but covered it well. "A pickpocket! I never would have guessed you were the type."

"Well, you know how we lower-class bints are. Can't keep our hands out of a man's pockets."

He looked even more startled and mumbled something about sexually aggressive women making him giddy.

"Touché" was the best she could think of to say. There was something about the man that kept her constantly off-balance.

"Care to tell me why you lifted my personal effects?" His light touch had vanished.

"You crashed a party where a man was murdered. I'm sorry, but I had to know if you were on the scene for some more nefarious purpose than stalking unsuspecting rich women."

"How is that any of your business?"

"I felt somewhat responsible for getting you in the door. So I had a look at your flat. Interesting hobby you've got."

"Ah, you found my trophy book!" His frown was instantly replaced with the proud grin of an enthusiast.

"You really put your heart and soul into it, don't you?" She didn't bother to hide her amusement, and he took no offense.

"It's a lark! The suspense of the entrance attempt! The constant fear of being discovered and turfed out."

"Speaking of suspense, how did you wind up in the library with that bump on your head?"

"I was curious what lay beyond the guard. So I spilled a cocktail on somebody and dragged the servant over to mop up. That gave me my chance to nip down the hall."

"Nosey bugger."

"I might say the same for you," was his none-too-sweet reply.

"Detecting is *my* hobby. Do go on."
"I came across this funny boxed-in stage."
"The diorama."
"Is that what it was? Anyway, there was only half of it in the hallway, so I looked for the other half. I heard something behind a door and went in."
"And found the other half."
"How did you know?"
"I came in a bit later and found you out cold and rolled up in a rug."
"Did you now?" His face took on an odd, quiet look, and he stared at her several moments without speaking. It was a very intent scrutiny that she felt down to her toes. "Just what is your game?" he finally asked.
"I told you, I'm playing detective. Just what is yours?"
"I'm a sportsman. You saw my trophies."
She let that go for the moment. "What did you see in the library besides the diorama?"
"Nothing at first, I was so taken with its realism. I'd never seen anything quite like it before, so I took a quick photo for my collection. Then I noticed Freddie Hardcastle passed out on the rug. It was a very fine Persian rug. While I was admiring its colours, I noticed our Freddie was breathing erratically. And I couldn't seem to find his pulse. The police were rather excited to hear about that."
"I bet. Did you happen to notice if there was a sword protruding from his chest?"
"Definitely not. I was leaning over him when I heard movement behind me. Then something hefty mashed me behind the ear." He grimaced at the memory.
"See who it was?"
"No, I was too enamoured of the colours of the rug; they were flashing like fireworks. Then I think somebody sneezed, but that could have been me."
"Was it a high-pitched sneeze or—"

"A deep, manly sneeze? I don't recall."

"Pity. It sounds to me like you blundered in before the murderer had a chance to finish Freddie off!"

"It looks that way, doesn't it? Next thing I knew I was in this godforsaken little hole with a nauseating headache."

"Oh, by the way, I'm having your film developed. Lucky the killer didn't nab your camera."

"He mustn't have known I had it; it was back in my pocket by the time he bashed my head in. I told the police about it, and they're dying to know who nicked it. They'll have a bone to pick with you, luv."

"They'll thank me when I hand over the film and remind them if I hadn't grabbed it, somebody less law abiding might have."

"I'm sure you'll soon have them eating out of your dainty hand," he crooned, a smirk lingering at the corner of his lips.

4

LETTIE STARTED HER INTERVIEWS with the footmen. Per Gwenna's instructions, they'd admitted guests only between the hours of seven and eight. Had anyone left the party between eight and nine o'clock? They shook their heads. No one had left early, and the footmen had resourcefully prevented anyone from leaving from the time the murder was discovered until the police arrived. Many of the guests had demanded to be permitted to leave, but the footmen had prevailed.

Lettie walked across the huge, echoing ballroom with Mrs. Batney as her guide. Here were the refreshment tables, the orchestra stage, and the diorama, exactly where it had been left after the discovery of the body. Lettie removed the sheet and made a careful examination. Where Freddie's corpse had lain was clearly marked by a rusty-looking stain of dried blood. There was more blood splattered across the stage and spilling over the side, staining the black frieze cloth that framed the bottom of the structure. Shakespeare looked a bit too coarse for Lettie's taste, although it could well be an accurate portrayal of an Elizabethan celebrity. The Dark Lady, on the other hand, was too pristine, the formula woman off the cover of a paperback romance—long raven hair, full scarlet cape, milky skin. The interpretation made the two characters seem at odds with one another and made Lettie uncomfortable.

When she had satisfied herself with the diorama, she turned her attention to the two balconies that graced the back wall of the ballroom. Mrs. Batney explained that the lower balcony opened off the first landing of the closed staircase and was where Bacon had manned the spotlamp. The higher one opened off of the second floor.

"And what is on the second floor?"

"Guest rooms, Penny's room, the beauty salon. The rest of the floor is used for storage," the secretary said.

"Were there any overnight guests?"

Mrs. Batney said there were not. Lettie then asked to see Monte, the servant who had stood guard over the corridor. He was most helpful, showing her where he had manned his post.

"Tell me, Monte, were you standing right here the entire evening?"

"That's right, just like I told the police. Except at half past eight, when I had to run over here and pick up the phone." He showed her where the phone was located.

"I see. That takes you out of the way of the hall. Now, when you were standing at your post, would you have been able to see anyone coming down the private stairs, or any activity inside the corridor itself?"

"Not without eyes in the back of my head."

Lettie went into the hallway, looked up the stairs, then down the hall to the French doors leading outside. "Could someone have gone out the back doors without your hearing them over the orchestra?"

Monte replied that he would have heard, all right. "Freddie locked up after Hal left and gave me the key. After that nobody could have gone out without the burglar alarm going off."

"Excellent. And who is Hal?"

"He's our stableboy. He helped carry the diorama into the library." Lettie nodded; that would explain the bit of manure Julia had found on the floor of the room.

Leonard Cheevers had built the diorama at the museum site (a house in Knightsbridge), constructing it in two separate pieces for easy transport. On the night of the party, Hal had driven a lorry to the museum and picked up the diorama, bringing it back to Castleberry. Bacon, Freddie, and Cheevers then helped Hal haul it in through the French doors, storing the main section in the library, the smaller part in the hall.

After questioning Monte and Bacon, Lettie drew up a timetable.

6:55 P.M.	Cheevers, Bacon & Freddie pass Monte and exit through the French doors to help Hal bring in the diorama.
7:15 P.M.	Cheevers and Bacon pass Monte on their way back to the party.
7:20 P.M.	Freddie gives Monte the back-door key, saying he's locked up after Hal, and returns to the party.
7:40 P.M.	Freddie passes Monte again on his way to his room on the third floor, remarking, "It's time to get into my pantyhose."
7:50 P.M.	Freddie returns in costume.
8:00 P.M.	Freddie gets up on stage, makes the announcement.

8:15 P.M. — Freddie passes Monte on his way back towards the stairs, saying he's got to change clothes before he drives all the women mad. Monte doesn't actually see if Freddie goes up the stairs.

8:30 P.M. — Phone call makes Monte leave post. Back in a few minutes.

8:45 P.M. — Max Genader lures Monte away again. Monte is gone about ten minutes while mopping up a spill. Killer might have run Freddie through and got back into ballroom before Monte returned. Does this make Max an accomplice— intentional or unwitting?

9:00 P.M. — Bacon and Monte go back down hall, quickly assemble diorama, pull it to entrance of ballroom. Bacon goes up to first balcony to man spotlamp. Turns off lights. Monte pulls diorama out into ballroom.
Killer could have returned to ballroom under cover of darkness at this time . . . if he didn't go upstairs? Could he have come down from upstairs, not from ballroom at all?

    Lettie stared up the steps for several minutes, considering the possibilities. Penny Smith admitted to being up there during the party, beavering away at her work. Penny was not a mixer: in fact she had a long-standing reputation in the house as a virtual recluse. She could have easily slipped down at any time and gone into the library without anyone seeing her. But did she have a motive for murder? Lettie sighed. So many suspects. She pocketed her notes and asked Mrs. Batney to show her where she might find Hal. As Lettie followed her guide through the garden, past the maze and fountains that could have held an Olympic swim meet, she continued asking questions.

"Who knew the diorama was going to be shown at the party?"

"I did," the secretary began, and ticked the rest off on her fingers. "Bacon, Monte, Hal. The mistress and her partners knew—Dr. Hoggwell and Sam Gary. Oh yes, Freddie and Cheevers, of course."

They crossed several acres of shrubs and flowers that were beginning to fade in the chill wind. Pausing to pass the time with a gardener who was tying up the zinneas, they learned that the lady of the house had just come this way a short while ago.

"She must have gone to the stables," Mrs. Batney said, taking the path to the paddock.

"Then I shall meet her at last!" Lettie cheerfully remarked, feeling her stomach constrict. She half expected to be snubbed or otherwise offended, but she was totally unprepared for the awful scene that met her eyes when Mrs. Batney pulled open the stable door.

Hardcastle's imposing figure filled the narrow entryway, the star of a grotesque drama taking place before a captive audience of horses whinnying in their stalls. Straw covered her billowing lavender chiffon dress. Bodice buttons were missing, her apricot curls askew. Beneath all the rouge and powder, murderous rage had turned her complexion an alarming shade of scarlet.

Lettie blinked, but could not take it in. Was two hundred pounds of rampaging Hardcastle really applying the business end of a riding crop to a screaming youth in torn denims? Or was there another, nicer interpretation? The scrap of lavender chiffon hanging from the weedy boy's teeth gave Lettie little hope that this spectacle was anything better than it appeared.

"Help! She's killing me!" the youth howled, trying to dodge the rain of blows.

One glance at the shocked secretary's face convinced Lettie that Mrs. Batney was in no shape to do anything but gape. Lettie would just have to rescue the boy herself. She squared her tiny shoulders and gingerly approached the combatants, timidly tapped Hardcastle on the back, and said, "I beg your pardon." This effectively distracted the berserk woman and gave her cringing victim a chance to tear free and run whimpering out the door.

Breathing heavily, Hardcastle turned to stare past them after the retreating youth. "How long has he worked here?" she demanded.

Mrs. Batney remained mute, so Lettie filled the gap. "I believe that was Hal the stableboy? Mrs. Batney told me that he's been working for you since he was a lad."

"Sooner or later they turn on you," Hardcastle declared, shaking straw from her dress. "Unstable stock, bad seed, years of inbreeding. Never turn your back on a servant, remember that!"

"I'm afraid it's the other way around in my household," Lettie twittered.

Gwenna focused on Lettie for the first time; her expression indicated she had no idea who this small silver-haired person was.

"Permit me to introduce myself; I'm Lettie Winterbottom. Your secretary has been showing me around."

"Kind of you to come," her hostess said as casually as if Lettie had accepted an invitation to tea. The mistress did, indeed, seem to change moods on the spot.

Lettie smiled cordially and studied the face underneath the apricot curls. Powder didn't hide the dark circles from too many sleepless nights. The latest face-lift had smoothed out but somehow emphasized the toll the years had taken. The dyed, elaborate hairdo was an undignified grasping after lost youth. Lettie found herself shrugging off years of prejudice, and feeling sorry for the old snob. "Please accept my deepest sympathy."

"What a nightmare!" Hardcastle shuddered. "I keep expecting to wake and find all is right again. All this nastiness done with. Freddie saddling up his favourite gelding and riding off with that silly wave of his . . ." Her voice broke and she quickly looked away.

Lettie murmured, "I understand," reluctant to come right out and demand to know why she'd been beating her stableboy with a riding crop. One hated to just blurt these things out, but one had to know.

Then Mrs. Batney came to Lettie's rescue, suddenly regaining her senses enough to quaver, "Were you murdering Hal?"

"Of course not!" her employer sniffed. "He tried to rape me. I had to defend myself."

"Indeed," Lettie politely mumbled, inwardly cringing and wondering what next. Before her hostess had a chance to brush past, Lettie cleared her throat and gingerly tested the waters. "I am working on a timetable of events surrounding the murder. Did you go down the hall at any time during the party? To check the diorama perhaps?"

Hardcastle fixed the detective with a frosty glare. "Of course not. A hostess's place is with her guests. I never left the ballroom for a minute."

"And when the diorama was wheeled in—how close were you standing to it?"

The question seemed to stab Hardcastle through the heart; she clutched her breast and closed her eyes. "Close enough" was her reply.

Lettie gently pressed on. "I know it's painful, but please try to remember—were you close enough to touch any part of it—"

"With my skirt, you mean?" The tone was bitter. "That's what the police kept asking. And I told them I'm certain I didn't touch it. I don't know how the blood got on my gown!"

This defiant statement ended the interview. Hardcastle swept away. Looking after her, Lettie thought she resembled a mannequin, wheels and pulleys propelling her jerkily but relentlessly towards the house that loomed in the background, as houses on the covers of Gothics always do.

5

NOT MUCH HAPPENED for a few hours. Hardcastle retired to her room with a headache, leaving Lettie free to wander about the house and gossip with the servants. Apparently no one felt compelled to feign sorrow at Freddie's passing. They were excited and repelled by his death, of course, but the general opinion was that even his grieving aunt would be better off without him. With no money of his own and no interest in earning any, Freddie had been a parasite with a new get-rich-quick scheme every week.

"He showed up a few years ago. An obvious bad egg, to my mind, but the mistress took her long-lost nephew under her wing. He'd been travelling the world and was stony broke. Good-for-nothing sharpies like that always are." Bacon instantly regretted this outburst of candour and refused to say another word.

Finding Janet Batney's office empty, Lettie took advantage of the opportunity to compare the type on the guest list with the type on Mrs. Batney's typewriter. The secretary walked in while Lettie was putting the cover back on the machine. "Why, Miss Winterbottom, what are you doing?" Mrs. Batney looked confused, even after she caught on. "Oh, the guest list."

"Yes. It was typed on this machine."

"As you have discovered, I never lock my office," Mrs. Batney said weakly.

"Perhaps you should," Lettie suggested. Sounds of commotion from the ballroom drifted through the open door. "What now?" Lettie wondered.

"I expect it's Cheevers come to take the diorama back to Knightsbridge."

Saying she was eager to meet him, Lettie left Mrs. Batney looking very defensive. In the ballroom Cheevers looked on while several servants moved in to unhinge the diorama. Although he was definitely seedy-looking, Lettie was quite taken with the artist. He had a sweet, humble manner and the air of one who'd never had a penny and had long ago given up worrying about it.

"The police are done with it," Cheevers told Lettie, tossing his head to get his unruly white hair out of his eyes. "And Gwenna understandably wants it out of her sight."

"It must have been awful to see your work put to such a foul purpose."

The artist frowned. "And who knows what will become of the project now."

"You think Dame Gwenna will lose all heart for it?"

He shrugged. "This is my first commission in years. I just hope this terrible business doesn't put an end to it."

As they pushed the diorama towards the door, the sheet slipped off. Cheevers stared at the bloodstains, then backed away and began to tremble. Bacon produced a tray of brandy, but the artist refused it, confessing to being a strict teetotaler.

"I don't know what's wrong with me," Cheevers apologised, as his colour returned.

The business of hauling out the diorama had attracted a crowd of observers, including Penny Smith, who clutched a writing pad to her chest as she leaned over the second-floor balcony rail and watched it go. Lettie noted the girl's dazed expression. Was she another onlooker who was moved by the sight of bloodstains? Only the lady of the house refrained from coming out to watch the scene of the crime being wheeled out the back door.

Nor did the appearance, later that afternoon, of the police inspector in charge of the case bring Gwenna Hardcastle out of her boudoir. Deputy Chief Inspector Thomas Alexander sent Bacon up with his respects and a request for an interview; the request was promptly denied.

The Inspector was a bulldog with the manner of a whippet—a jumpy sort with an incongruously high-pitched voice coming out of a big, square face. Part of his tetchiness apparently stemmed from an instinctive dread of cases involving the peerage. Postponing another attempt to interview the Great One, he confessed to Lettie over a cup of tea in the Amber Room. He had acquired his wariness twenty years before, when he first joined the force and became involved in the famous Duke of Wainscoting murder investigation. "Every time I turned around I was treading on another diamond-encrusted toe."

"And Dame Gwenna won't be making it any easier on you," Lettie commiserated.

"A real prima donna, that one."

"And volatile when provoked." She described the tussle in the stable. "She said he'd tried to . . . molest her." Lettie reddened and stared up at the ceiling, which was covered with a mob of painted cherubs infesting a mountain of puffy clouds. There was something decidedly obscene about your average cherub; and these were fatter and more pious than usual, their eyes rolling heavenwards. Her own eyes returned to earth, where Alexander was choking on his tea. "Are you all right, Inspector?"

"Let me get this straight. That skinny little bloke of a stableboy was molesting her?"

Lettie nodded, and looked at the floor. No cherubs here. Pity; it would have been fun to tread on a few.

"She's old enough to be his grandmother, isn't she?" He groaned. "But then, maybe it fits." A tormented frown stole over his face. When pressed, he would only say, "She writes novels crammed with sex, doesn't she? Strikes me as damned unhealthy for a lady at her time of life."

She sensed from his increasing agitation that there was something more on his mind, a matter he wasn't looking forward to handling. Playing a hunch, she offered to deal with Gwenna. "I'd be glad to serve as go-between. I believe she's determined not to talk to you."

Emotions played across his homely face. First he was a drowning man about to grasp gratefully the lifeline she'd just tossed him. But then he glumly decided to weather the rough seas on his own, or die in the attempt. "Give me a simple street mugging any day," he lamented, tucking into a tray of watercress sandwiches with the desperate concentration of a famine victim.

"I hope you know you may rely on me to do everything I can to facilitate your investigation." She was careful to balance her reassuring tone with respect. "I've had some experience in detection, in a small way."

"I read the papers, Miss Winterbottom," he said quietly. He might let the old girl have her bit of fun. Who knows, maybe she'd come up with something useful. "You did a tidy job of work on the Stonehenge case, though I can't say much for your choice of partners on that one."

"He chose me," she replied, hiding a reminiscent smile. Dear John David! He had a remarkable talent for putting the authorities' noses out of joint. She hadn't heard from her erstwhile colleague in a while and wondered where he was. Probably in a jail halfway round the globe. With an effort she shook free of remembered adventures and returned to the present case. "Tell me, have you found the missing glass from the study liquor cabinet?"

His droopy eyes grew round with respect. "So you know about that! Would you care to tell me how?"

She explained that her niece had been in the murder room for a few moments and taken a quick look around. "She's very observant."

He gave her a slightly fishy look and said he'd better talk to this niece. She said Julia would be coming by within the hour and again inquired about the missing glass.

"We found it in the punchbowl. The alcohol took care of any prints." He downed the last of his tea and got to his feet.

She began to rattle on, determined to get some answers before letting him get away. "The maid says all the glasses were in place when she dusted on the day of the party. Bacon claims that the study door was locked when he and the others brought the diorama into the adjoining library. So it was unlocked sometime during the party. That's when somebody brought the glass out and dropped it into the punchbowl."

Saying it wasn't a bad theory, he volunteered that the small amount of blood on the study carpet was indeed from the deceased. There were minute fragments of scalp tissue and blood on the crystal Scotch decanter, indicating that the killer struck Freddie with it, knocking him to the floor, alive but unconscious. Then he was dragged into the library, lifted into the diorama and fatally stabbed.

"I don't know why the killer brought the glass out to the party with him, but I have some thoughts about what

Freddie might have been doing in Gwenna's study," she said. "Suppose Freddie was behind the practical jokes that have been plaguing his aunt. Breaking into her study might have been just another way to annoy her. She's very protective of that room, I understand—watching the maid while she dusts, not letting anyone else in."

Alexander shifted his weight back and forth, fingering something inside his breast pocket. "Freddie plays nasty tricks. Gwenna catches him at it, is enraged by the betrayal . . ." He stared down at Lettie. "You're sure you actually saw her beat the stableboy?" She answered in the affirmative. He set his jaw, excused himself, and purposefully marched out. She could hear him instructing Bacon to inform the mistress that since she wouldn't come down, he had no choice but to interview her in her boudoir.

Lettie discreetly followed and planted her ear against the bedroom door a moment after the policeman used a skeleton key to enter. His trespass produced a war whoop from Gwenna, but he bravely held his ground.

Bacon sauntered down the hall, never batting an eyelash at Lettie in her classic eavesdropping pose. In the next few moments, it seemed like everyone on the staff found an urgent errand that required passing that door. But with the strategic listening post already occupied, they all had to go about their business. If they'd had any inkling of the rude stuff Lettie was hearing, they might have shamelessly shoved the old lady out of the way.

The first shocker had to do with an anonymous packet of information the police had received in the mail; it had convinced the Inspector that Freddie hadn't been Gwenna's nephew at all. Gwenna hooted in outraged disbelief, but soon changed her tune, apparently persuaded by the documents themselves. During the ensuing dangerous silence, Lettie turned her head, to give her numb ear a rest.

Then Gwenna rambled emotionally for a while. It seemed impossible! How could it be? It came out little by little that she had not seen her nephew since he was a child, just before he'd emigrated with his parents to New Zealand. But Gwenna claimed she had recognised him when he showed up in London two years ago. He was a bit short of cash, so she took him in. He resembled his mother enough that Gwenna didn't think to question his identity.

"You never suspected he could have been an imposter?" The uneasy timbre of Alexander's voice made Lettie wonder. Was it possible that the *real* bombshell hadn't been dropped yet?

"I had every reason to believe he was my sister's son. He seemed to know everything he should—the intimate things a stranger wouldn't know. Of course, I'd been estranged from his parents for years . . . but I remember quite a bit about them."

The Inspector cleared his throat. "One other thing came with these documents. This photograph."

There was an awful scream. Then silence. Lettie fidgeted, tempted to fling open the door and rush in.

Then something shattered against the door. The Inspector shouted something incomprehensible. Heavier objects thudded against wood and plaster, knocking a painting off the wall a few inches from Lettie's shoulder. As she jumped back, the door flew open and the Inspector burst out, his face white, a photo falling from his hand. It fluttered to the floor, and Lettie was on it in a second. Her jaw, for the first time in her life, actually dropped open. There were Gwenna and Freddie, cosy as two bugs. In bed together.

"It could have been faked," Lettie told the Inspector when they were once again in the relative safety of the Amber Room. She was recovering from the shock more quickly than he was, from the looks of him. "Her eyes are closed. She might have been drugged, unaware of what was happening."

He practised his breathing and tried not to think about it. Why did he let things upset him so? Perhaps the Missus was right—he was too sensitive to be a cop. He involuntarily shuddered. He wouldn't soon forget the awful spectre of unleashed Hardcastle wrath. The sound of a footfall startled him out of his dazed funk. He grabbed the photo and stuffed it into his pocket as Bacon came in to announce that Mr. Montegue, society photographer from *The Sun*, was waiting to speak to Inspector Alexander.

Glancing around the card table at the absorbed expressions of Mrs. Batney, Inspector Alexander, and Norton Montegue, Lettie was reminded of these dreadful six months of her life when she belonged to a bridge club. They had just begun studying the photographs Montegue had taken the night of the party when Bacon showed Julia in.

Lettie introduced her around as Julia pulled up a chair to join them. A hundred or so guests had been photographed entering the party. Lots of influential faces, but after Julia had looked at a few dozen swells posing in the same foyer, her eyes began to glaze over. Too bad Max wasn't here; he'd have no doubt relished endlessly goggling at the rich and famous. "Why snap everybody walking in the door?" she asked the photographer.

Montegue's oversized nose twitched in his deeply lined face as he wearily said it was one of the hostess's commandments. At a Hardcastle affair, guests were admitted only during a one-hour period. And the photographer had better catch every grand entrance, or there would be hell to pay. "It got bloody dull hanging about in the foyer, believe me," he drawled.

Julia commiserated. She liked his odd looks. His

short neck and stocky build made him appear wider than he was tall. His weathered face gave him an outdoorsy appearance one didn't usually associate with society photographers. He'd acquired that look from spending the first half of his life big game hunting in India and Africa, he told Julia. In those days his family had still had enough money to pay for his amusing tramps all over the globe, rifle slung over his shoulder, flasks of gin and quinine water in his bush jacket. And now he passed his autumn years camped inside foyers, shooting party guests with his Nikon. It was altogether too bloodless.

"And this must be Max Genader," Lettie said, picking up the photo of Julia and the attractive stranger. She stared hard at the man's dark eyes. Just where did this smiling devil fit in?

"Ah, I remember that one," Montegue said. "He was at the Flushingdale soirée a few weeks ago. Nobody seemed to know who he was."

"Don't look at me," Julia protested. "I don't either."

"First date?" the Inspector asked, eyeing her suspiciously.

"Something like that," she replied.

"Here are the Huntfords," Mrs. Batney said. "He's a big name in infrared, I believe. She's cousin to Prince Philip." Between the secretary and the photographer, they eventually got everyone identified and labelled. Julia perked up when they got to look at something other than the same potted palm beside the door. Montegue had moved into the ballroom in time to catch Freddie making his announcement. These candid snaps were definitely more interesting. Freddie hamming it up in that silly costume. Dr. Hoggwell chatting up an important military man while Benecia Hoggwell looked bored blue.

"And now for my grisly masterpieces," Montegue sighed, unveiling the pictures of the body and the frantic aftermath. An overwrought Gwenna doing a fair rendition of a demented Lady Macbeth in her bloodstained gown. Studies of people's reactions ranging from embarrassment to horror. Cheevers gripping a drink in his hand, a dazed grimace twisting his lips.

"Cheevers told me he didn't drink," Lettie said. Janet Batney said she thought he didn't.

"Can't blame him for making an exception," the photographer remarked.

Inspector Alexander made a soft noise in his throat as he leaned over to study Cheever's photo. Julia moved a little closer and stared at the glass in the artist's hands; there was something off about it . . . it didn't match the party crystal, but she'd seen it before. Of course, the missing glass from the study! There was no doubt that the Inspector twigged to it too. Julia answered Lettie's inquiring look with one that promised to tell all later.

"Just a few more." Montegue passed out the last pile.

Julia's eyes were immediately drawn to an extraordinary-looking man whom she'd never seen before. He was standing beside two couples. The women were crying on each other's shoulders while their men looked uncomfortable. A few paces away stood a droll old elf in his late fifties. His eyes were big and blue, his cheeks very rosy above a red cupid's-bow mouth. With his white hair and bulging middle, he looked uncannily like the popular depictions of Saint Nick, but without the beard. Only this Santa (in a burgundy velvet tux) was sly instead of merry. She asked who he was, half expecting to hear he was Killer Kringle, Kris Kringle's evil brother. Mrs. Batney told her she was looking at a picture of Sam Gary, the infamous third partner.

"How did a wrong number like him get to be partners with Hardcastle?" Julia asked, rephrasing the very question she'd overheard at the party.

The secretary said Dr. Hoggwell had brought him into the deal. Montegue added his two bits. "I understand

Gary was one of Hoggwell's patients. The doctor helped him lose fifty pounds. Now he's got a chance to lose several thousand, if things keep going sour."

Respecting Montegue as an excellent source of gossip, Lettie asked him if he thought the deal might fall through.

"If Gwenna's mental state doesn't improve, *I* wouldn't want to invest in it. Not that I have any spare cash," he lightly added, then grew serious. "Some people say Gwenna killed Freddie. I don't believe it for a minute. That little tear-away meant the world to her."

Lettie and the Inspector shared a look that was duly noted and silently speculated over by the others. Julia could hardly wait to get the old girl alone to compare notes.

"Any idea when we may publish these?" Montegue asked the Inspector. Thus far there had only been a paragraph in the papers, details to be released by the police at a later time. "My editor's eager, to put it mildly." He stacked them in five neat piles and slid them into a large envelope.

Alexander took the envelope and dismissed him with a promise to release them as soon as possible. Lettie began to plot how she was going to get a set of copies for herself.

When Montegue had left and Mrs. Batney gone off on an errand, Julia waved a chemist's envelope under the Inspector's nose, explaining it contained yet another set of snapshots—these developed from the film she'd removed from Max Genader's camera. This announcement precipitated some heavy weather. The Inspector took noisy umbrage to her removing evidence and made sullen reference to fines and imprisonment.

They let him cut up rough for a while, then calmed him down with the argument that her interference might have prevented the evidence from falling into criminal hands. Peace restored, they put their heads together over this new batch of photos, which inclued Dr. Hoggwell among other famous faces, as well as a picture of the diorama in the library before Freddie had been put there and run through. Nothing struck them as particularly enlightening about this new batch—but then, they'd had enough photos for one day, if not a lifetime.

Muttering something about starting his own scrapbook, the Inspector left the room, and the two women ran for the front door. They'd have to rush to get a chance to talk to Cheevers before the police nabbed him. Speeding down the drive, Julia told Lettie about the telltale photo of Cheevers holding the wrong kind of glass.

"That does look bad for the poor man," Lettie agreed.

"Sounds like you think he's innocent."

"Things are getting so complicated, I hardly know what I think anymore." Lettie described Gwenna's run-in with the stableboy and the pornographic photo of her and Freddie.

Julia almost swerved off the road at this last bit of information, and had to laugh in disbelief when Lettie added, "And it turns out Freddie wasn't really her nephew."

"You're joking!"

When Julia finally ran out of surprised expletives, Lettie posed a question that had been troubling her. "Who could coach an imposter for that role? It would have to be a close friend of Gwenna's sister . . . or . . ."

"A relative," Julia supplied. "Like Tony or Benecia Hoggwell."

Conversation lagged for a while until Julia had successfully navigated an especially thick clot of traffic. They passed a park where leaves rattled in restless swirls across the fading green grass. Grey clouds heaped up in the sky. The day was taking a decided turn for the dramatic.

"Let's see if I can get this mess sorted out in my brain," Julia said when she'd pulled away from the pack. "First, what about this scene with the stableboy?"

"Hal. He either sexually attacked his employer, as she claims, or he did something else to earn himself a beating by her hand."

"Could he just have forgotten to pull his forelock enough in the presence of his betters?"

"I think it has to do with the murder. He might know something and was trying to blackmail his employer. In which case she may have pummeled that idea out of him."

Changing the subject, Lettie told her about the timetable she'd worked out.

Julia listened, then asked, "How do we know that Hal really went out the back? Freddie might have lied about that if he and Hal were up to something."

"Precisely my thought. Then they had a disagreement that ended in Freddie's . . ."

"Demise. Right. But where did he go afterwards? Surely he would have been noticed in the ballroom, unless he was wearing a dinner jacket. You did say he looked a bit rustic?"

"Decidedly. Perhaps he went up the stairs and hid."

"Who else was upstairs at that time?"

"Just Penny Smith, Gwenna's young researcher. She might have heard Hal run by, or even seen him. That would explain why she is so nervous . . ." Lettie fidgeted, wishing she had brought some knitting; it always helped her reasoning process. "But let us assume for a moment that Hal just innocently went out the back and had nothing to do with the crime. As the only person upstairs during the party, Penny Smith had the opportunity to get to and from the murder room without being observed by the guard, who had his back to her."

"Yes, I see what you mean." Julia looked thoughtful. "And what about her motive?"

"I gather Freddie was universally disliked."

Julia said she'd seen enough of him to understand why.

"And there's no doubt in my mind that Penny is terribly upset about something."

"Murder aside, working for Gwenna Hardcastle must be upsetting enough. And how did *you* and the Most High get on?" Julia teased.

Lettie wrinkled her nose. "We haven't actually talked for more than five minutes since I arrived. Thus far she's been in a rage, indisposed, and in a panic—in that order."

Julia gave her a curious look. "That sounded noticeably less acerbic than your former references to the Princess of Passion. Has Her Highness won you over?"

"Hardly!" The older woman laughed. "But I can't help feeling sorry for her."

"Do you think she's bonkers?"

"Hysterical—but who wouldn't be?"

"Yes, this whole business is taking on a definitely lurid cast. Could she and Freddie really have been lovers?" Julia asked, thinking that was one photo she would gladly forego examining.

Lettie admitted that the very idea struck her as completely preposterous. But that might be just her own sensibilities revolting at the thought.

6

THE SITE OF THE FUTURE Hardcastle Museum of Historical Romance was a textbook example of Georgian architecture—a solid, three-storied house with a large rose garden that had recently been trimmed down to naked stems just above the ground.

It took several rings of the doorbell to bring the sound of approaching feet. Then the lanky figure of Cheevers was bowing in the doorway, his hair and frayed woollen shirt powdered with sawdust.

After Lettie introduced Julia, Cheevers asked if they'd come for the grand tour. He sounded jolly, but seemed almost relieved to see them. Julia wondered if he'd been expecting the police. "Well, come in, it'll make a welcome break for me."

Lettie said, "So glad we're not imposing."

The first thing they noticed upon entering the hall was a life-sized portrait of Gwenna as the Lady of Shalott. If they had not read the placard, they never would have recognised the character, who traditionally was depicted as a slimmer, younger woman. "A good likeness," Lettie mumbled, at loss for a more original comment.

"I prefer the Waterhouse version, myself," Cheevers

remarked, not bothering to feign admiration for this inferior work.

"It isn't very good, is it?" Julia said, gazing up at the familiar face made absurd by the artist's desperate attempts to lend romantic soulfulness to Hardcastle's domineering features.

"What we artists will sometimes do for money," their guide moaned, and on that ironic note began showing them around, explaining that every room was to be designed around its own diorama, with furnishings and artifacts appropriate to the historical period.

"A decorator's dream job!" Lettie said wistfully. Who wouldn't kill for the chance? "Who's been commissioned to do it?"

"Gwenna is apparently having trouble finding a designer she can work with." His voice was gently sarcastic.

"Come along, I've got the Robin Hood piece done. It's right this way." He showed them into what used to be a drawing room, but was now bare of furnishings except for a diorama. The visitors sincerely admired its composition. Leaning against a gnarled oak, a raven-haired Maid Marion was transfixed by the sight of her Robin, his face alight with manly passion as he came galloping down the dell towards her. It was mostly in blues and grey-greens, with lots of rich, leafy shadows that were admirably integrated.

"I suspect Gwenna loves this one!" Lettie sighed. "It's charming."

The artist modestly admitted, "It's my best treatment of light and shadow." He ran his hand through his thick hair to get it off his forehead. "Gwenna thinks there aren't enough warm shades."

Julia shook her head in disgust. "That would ruin it."

"My reaction exactly," he said, obviously still relishing a battle won.

He showed them two other completed dioramas, saying twenty more were planned. When they asked to see the fatal one, he obligingly took them down to the west wing, explaining, "I'm avoiding this one. Frankly, I'd like to disassemble it, after all that's happened."

"But it should draw the crowds," Julia said. Her cynicism plainly discomfited the creator. "Everyone will want to see the famous demise-en-scène."

Lettie circled the diorama, lifted the skirt and noted the forty inches between the base and the floor, then studied it from every angle. She asked which sides were facing the library that night. Julia pointed them out, and Lettie resumed her intense scrutiny.

"May I step inside? I would be most careful," Lettie promised, her elderly face managing to look appealingly like a child's.

"I'd rather you didn't. I hope you understand—the thing is fragile. If it turns out that its fate is to be dismantled, I shall let you climb all over it first, if you like."

"I understand." Lettie tried not to show her disappointment. "Tell me, are both figures movable?"

He nodded. "I like to keep them freestanding to facilitate cleaning and maintenance." At that point in their conversation, the jingling of a phone echoed somewhere in the empty house. "Blasted contraption," he grumbled and trotted off to answer it.

Lettie saw her chance and wasted no time climbing into the diorama, telling Julia, "Keep a look out, will you?"

"Be careful!" Julia warned, obediently taking up a post near the door. "If he comes back and Shakespeare's lying on his face, he's going to be suspicious."

"I'm terribly rude," Lettie acknowledged, staring up into the Bard's face, who stood slightly taller than her five feet two inches. His costume was exquisite, his face so lifelike she could almost smell the liquor on his breath.

It took only a couple of steps to cross the stage. Now

inside the scene, she became aware of the optical tricks the artist had skillfully used to convince the viewer that he was perceiving a much deeper space than actually was there. She scanned the background, trying to decide how to get up onto the balcony without using the flimsy-looking trellis. She tapped a low wall running very close to the facade of the Dark Lady's house. It felt and sounded solid enough.

"You're not planning to climb up there, are you?" Julia said doubtfully, nervously keeping one eye on her irrepressible aunt and the other eye on the hall. "It might be better if I did it."

"Don't worry, it's not as high as it looks from over there." She raised herself up, grasping the railing and easing onto the balcony. The railing was about sixteen inches high, the balcony behind it less than two feet deep and five feet long, although it appeared much roomier. It was constructed of heavy lumber and seemed to be well supported by the entire structure, as sturdy as a real house.

Lettie half expected the Dark Lady to turn and look at this untimely intrusion. But the Lady just kept gazing under her thick lashes at her lover below. The mannequin's purple velvet skirt filled the width between the railing and the facade of the building, effectively cutting the balcony in half. Lettie gently touched the skirt; there seemed to be an iron petticoat underneath. Lifting up the skirt revealed a hooped cylinder instead of feet and legs. "The Lady isn't what she seems," Lettie said. "I imagine she's designed this way to be more stable. How very clever." The cylinder had hinges and would fold flat when pressure was applied.

"He's coming back," Julia warned.

Lettie leapt down and was innocently admiring the view from the front window when Cheevers came striding in. "Sorry to run off like that. Let me show you what I'm presently working on."

They followed him into a large room at the back of the house that served as his studio. It was piled high with wire, timbers, bags of clay and plaster, paint, and various other materials as well as all sorts of tools. The work in progress looked like the skeleton of a garden shed, but it would soon be transformed into a castle turret for Launcelot and Guinevere. He showed them the sketches detailing measurements and visual relationships from various points of view. It was all very mathematical, and Lettie didn't understand a word of it, although she bubbled, "This is so interesting! One never even dreams of how much goes into something . . ." She trailed off, looking up at him. He seemed like such a decent sort. Was it just an act? There was only one way to find out. "I am concerned about you, Mr. Cheevers. You're in a very precarious position, as you're doubtless aware."

Clearly taken aback, he asked her what she was referring to. "If you mean the future of the project, I have been worried about that myself. If Gwenna should cancel the whole thing . . ."

"You'd be out of a job," Julia interjected. "Where would that leave you?"

"Well, according to our contract, I'd be paid for whatever dioramas I'd completed. And if the partners were the ones to cancel, I'd get almost a thousand pounds in severance pay." He cleared his throat, nervously looking from one to the other, trying to estimate their reactions.

"And if you just quit?"

"Then I would get no severance," came his reluctant reply. He could see what they were thinking.

Julia said, "I gather you haven't found working with Gwenna to be an ideal situation." Was that a strong enough motive to kill Freddie? Escape from an intolerable situation with a nice bonus to tide him over.

"That doesn't mean I'm a killer," he declared, picking up a hammer and tapping it lightly against his thigh. Julia edged closer to the timber pile, in case the need for a weapon should arise. Lettie, on the other hand, gave no indication of anticipating any problems.

"The police have a photo of you holding the telltale glass right after the body was discovered," Lettie quietly told him.

He sighed and grew very calm, as if she'd just advised him to expect rain. He put aside the hammer and picked up a hacksaw, saying, "Thank you for warning me." He silently studied the blade for a short while before continuing. "I wasn't certain the camera had got me. Just my luck, caught holding a glass of blood."

"Blood!" Julia exclaimed.

She couldn't decide what to make of it until Lettie said, "Oh dear, that does look bad."

But he had an explanation. "The lights were out. The diorama had just been brought in. I felt a glass being shoved into my hand. There was no place to set it down, so I just held onto it. There was a terrible outcry over the body. The lights came on. People were in a panic. Somebody pointed at the blood on Gwenna's skirt. I'd been carrying the glass around for a few minutes before I happened to notice what it contained." He stopped his recitation to make an apologetic gesture. "I didn't know what to do. So I dumped it into the punchbowl as casually as I could, hoping that in the confusion no one would notice."

Lettie pointed out that the police might think he had slipped back down the hall while the servant was gone and killed Freddie, using the glass to bring some of the blood out to the ballroom, where he spilled it on Gwenna.

He sat down on a box and let the saw fall from his hand. It hit the floor with a clang that echoed with a hollow finality. "How do I prove I'm innocent?" he asked, burying his face in his hands.

Promising to help in any way they could, they soon left him alone. On their way out the street they passed a police car.

"The best thing he's got going for him is motive," Julia said. "He's not the type to kill someone in the hope of driving his employer mad and thereby getting out of an unpleasant job with a thousand pounds' severance pay."

Lettie agreed that in itself it wasn't much of a motive. But suppose the police found witnesses who claimed Cheevers loathed the Hardcastles? "You know how damning a mere argument can sound."

It was starting to drizzle when Julia dropped Lettie off in front of Castleberry. The younger woman announced her plans to go snoop around Sam Gary's junkyard. Maybe she'd get lucky and meet the great man himself.

"Be careful," Lettie told her. She would really have preferred to do that chore herself. It was worrisome to watch a pretty niece go off to meet a gangster.

7

It was the end of the road for dear old Agnes. A giant metal talon descended from the sky and pierced her sides with iron fingers. She shuddered, resisting only for a moment before being plucked into the air. As she tilted, her glasses shattered, bits raining down on the oozing, rain-soaked soil below. The nose-heavy angle made her seat come loose and lodge halfway out the door.

Into the waiting maw she fell, released from the grip of the plucking machine. Fluids poured from her vitals. Chuffing and horrible groans rumbled all around her. The metal walls vibrated, then began to close in. But just as her skeleton started to crumble there was a reprieve.

Bert got down out of the cab of his crane and joined Jake at the edge of the crusher. Below them, glistening in the drizzle, Agnes's half-crumpled body lay wedged into the chamber. Jake pushed his hardhat back on his head. He was a very greasy character with a cut lip and blackened eye. "Damn tough little bangers, them Austins. Owned one myself."

"From the looks a them tatty seats, somebody lived in this one." Bert grunted as he leaned forward for a better view. "Best get down there and look. Motor block's probably jammed in the corner.

Jake wasn't having any. "Not on yer life! You remember what happened to the last bloke what got down there wid a prybar. Wound up a cube about this big." He measured off a shape the size of a cereal box.

Bert shrugged. "Made it easier to ship 'em home, didn't it? Now git yer arse down there."

"Never."

"You'll do as I say."

"Sam's the boss," Jake grumbled. "Get *him* to go in there. He's the one won't buy a new crusher."

"I'll tell him yer suggestion." Bert threw down his gloves in disgust and climbed off the big machine. He crossed the wrecking yard with the easy confidence of a man who thought nothing of knackering a five-ton goods van and a dozen autos before lunch. Rain beaded on the heaps of rusted metal: old iceboxes, mattress springs, bicycles, railroad rolling stock, ancient earthmovers. He sloshed through the muck, oblivious to the pools of dark water skimmed by oily rainbows of colour, rounded a corner, and almost walked right into Julia. Losing a slight amount of his self-possession, Bert unconsciously wiped his stained boiler suit and touched his cap.

"Hullo," Julia said. "I seem to be lost. The man at the gate said to turn left at the brake drums." She pointed quizzically at the piles of axles.

"That'd be over there a ways. Lookin' for the office, dearie?" She said she was. "Then follow me, it's just past that pile of Cortinas." He gave her his best toothless smile and looked her over. He'd never been this close to such a classy bird and wondered what sort of underwear she was wearing.

But all such thoughts were driven from Bert's head when he stepped inside the office door and the boss jumped on him with both feet. "You jammed the effin' machine again, didn't you? Bloody hell, how many . . ."

Sam Gary's tirade stopped when Julia caught his eye. "Who's the twist?" he asked Bert.

"I'm Julia Carlisle. Reporter for *The Sun*," she volunteered, staring in fascination at his remarkable face.

Sam Gary's normally cagey eyes got a little cagier as he looked her up and down. He'd never talked to a reporter before, but they wrote dirt about him now and again. Nothing they could actually prove, but it irked him just the same. "Come to rag Sam Gary have you? Another lying bitch out to slander a poor workin' man. Christ, it makes me want to puke."

"Don't do that," she begged. "Just tell a poor working girl about your association with Dr. Hoggwell. I understand you used to be a patient of his." Next to her, Bert looked interested, caught his boss's glare, and studiously stared out the soot-caked little window.

Surprisingly, Sam Gary laughed, which set his stomach shaking—almost like a bowl full of jelly. "You want to know how a crusty old so-and-so like me got up with the nabobs. Well, popsie, I got no time for standin' around. I got to get my yard men straight."

She followed them through the yard, twice having to break into a trot to keep up with their pace through the mud. Thank God for PVC boots, she thought.

She scaled the ladder and joined Sam Gary and Bert at the top. Returning with a six-foot prybar, Jake stopped to leer at her. "Stop gogglin' and get down in there!" Sam barked. Jake hesitated and Sam scowled menacingly. "Go on, you mealy-mouthed little gut bag, or I'll kick yer face in."

"But you remember what happened ta—"

"He didn't move fast enough," Sam said carelessly. "You want to clear out now, or are you goin' down there?"

The two men stared at each other; then Jake reluctantly turned, leaped down onto Agnes's top, gingerly working his way forward using the prybar as a staff. Bert headed for the control box, where a collection of levers and cranks controlled the hydraulic ram that did the crushing. Sam Gary balanced on the side, ready to relay signals. "All right, Bert, now back her up!"

Air sighed out, a compressor started up. The ram bucked, heaved, pulled back. Julia started as the old Austin jumped, nearly dumping Jake over the spot that had once been the bonnet. Sam Gary glanced at her, then pulled a pack of Players from his pocket. "It'll take a minute to clear it up. So I got some time for you, dolly." His insinuating sneer would have been offensive coming from anyone. It was doubly intolerable on the face she'd grown up associating with the sweet old saint who delivered all the goodies on Christmas Eve.

"I'll tell you what brings uppish blokes to the humble likes of Sam Gary." He reached into the pocket of his dirty sweater and brought out a fat wallet, pulled out a sheaf of bills, and tickled her cheek with them. She tried to push his hand away, and took a step down the ladder to get away from him. "Always keep a bit of cash on me. In case I see somethin' I want. And that's what it's all about—cash."

Julia thought about it. The rumours about this crook, his ties to loansharking, gambling, who knew what else. "Did you loan money to Freddie Hardcastle?"

He chuckled in a way calculated to make her even more uncomfortable and sidestepped her question. "Let's just say I'm a friend of the family. The old Queenie wanted herself a fancy museum. It sounded like a good thing, so I offered to go along."

Apparently forgetting her existence, he glanced down at Jake levering away at the remains of Agnes's four cylinders. Sam suddenly turned and signalled Bert, who obediently pulled a set of levers. Propelled by five hundred tons of pressure, the ram moved forward. Jake let out a scream, jumped back, and fell. Julia shouted a warning, but Jake was all too aware of his danger. He scrambled over the bent panels of the old saloon and slipped on the roof, one leg going through the rear window. The noise was tremendous now as sheet metal smoked and screeched under the pressure of the crusher. But Sam Gary just puffed his cigarette and calmly observed as Jake desperately wrenched at his trapped leg.

Julia ran to Bert and yelled in his ear. Bert grabbed at the release, but there was a built-in delay while valves took time to close. The ram continued to move in as Jake, pants torn, popped up over the side, scrabbling across the metal grates of the walkway and out of danger. The enormous engine of destruction sighed to a stop.

Julia turned on Sam Gary and told him just what she thought of him. The demon Santa simply grinned. And she understood that the demonstration had really been for her benefit. He had, in his own subtle way, given her a message: don't mess with Sam Gary.

Fighting for control of her temper, she went down the ladder and marched in the direction of the gate. Once safely out of sight, she headed back towards the ramshackle structure that served as the office. A quarrel of seagulls looked down from a mountain of rubbish that rose behind the shack, impressive as the Alps towering above a tiny mountain cabin.

She hurriedly shuffled through the papers on the desk but didn't see anything that didn't have something to do with salvage. Under a pile of receipts, however, she found an interesting brochure for Godive, a health spa in Marseilles specialising in weight control and something called "habit management." It promised "absolute discretion in a gorgeous holiday setting." She stuffed it into her pocket and ran for the gate.

The Hardcastle residence was very quiet when Lettie returned shortly before dinnertime. "Any new developments?" she asked Bacon, as he took her coat. His manner became even more circumspect than usual as he informed her that she'd just missed meeting Dr. Hoggwell. Apparently Mrs. Batney had details on his visit. Lettie wasted no time looking up the secretary.

She found Janet Batney at her desk, labouring over the house accounts. The secretary eagerly dropped her pencil as Lettie pulled up a chair. "The mistress was having one of her bad days," Janet began, launching into her tale. "Inspector Alexander's visit had so disturbed her that she had me call Dr. Hoggwell. She's come to rely on him so much lately." But the doctor didn't have his usual soothing effect; Mrs. Batney heard the shouting clear across the hall. "They were in the library, so when I heard the commotion, I went into the conservatory and listened at the connecting door." She looked properly embarrassed. "I suppose I shouldn't have, but I felt it my duty."

"You did the right thing." Lettie's words were heartfelt. Eavesdropping was vital to solving any case. There was hardly any better way to find things out.

Encouraged, the secretary proceeded to describe what she had overheard. Gwenna had said she didn't know how much more she could take; the news she'd gotten that day had been utterly devastating. "I need you, Tony. Please, don't you turn against me, too!"

The doctor had said she'd have to pull herself together, that rumours of her deteriorating health were all over town. He had named a psychiatrist friend who could do her a world of good, if she'd only give him a chance.

"I don't need a psychiatrist!" Gwenna had screamed. "Tony, listen. I just found out Freddie wasn't really my nephew!"

"That's what she said." Mrs. Batney's dramatic pause was somewhat wasted on Lettie. "Can you credit it? It must have thrown Dr. Hoggwell for a loop, because he didn't say anything for the longest time." She was obviously relishing relating the information, unaware that it was old news to her audience. Lettie wondered if it had also been old news to Hoggwell. "But the worst was about a photo. Of the mistress and Freddie, stripped to their you-know-whats. In bed together!" Beads of perspiration had appeared on the secretary's high, narrow forehead. It would be some time before that bit of news no longer got her pulse going. It was unthinkable, but she hadn't been able to stop thinking about it for a moment. "She said it was faked, of course."

Hoggwell got very excited then too. He had said it had to be kept quiet. After all, there was the future of the museum project to consider. It was the Hardcastle good name that would carry it. But not if that name was tainted with rumours of perversion, insanity, murder . . .

"That's a strange tack to take," Lettie interjected. "I mean, everybody knows that rumours of perversion, et cetera would probably guarantee the project's success. It would be in all the tabloids and the crowds would queue up for days . . ." She trailed off, stunned by this new possibility. Was it all just part of some diabolical publicity stunt?

Janet resumed her narrative. Gwenna hadn't liked the doctor's comments, had gotten hysterical, rambling on about a plot to send her over the edge. "Who are they? Why are they doing this to me?" she had sobbed.

"It was just pathetic," the secretary confided. "I never thought I'd ever pity that woman like I do. She used to be so independent. For all her faults, I had to admire her for that."

There wasn't much more to tell. The doctor had finally given Gwenna something to calm her down and had gone away.

Lettie thanked Mrs. Batney for the information and went in search of her employer. Perhaps assuring Gwenna that someone was on her side would be of some small comfort. But when she found Gwenna in the library, she was in no shape to be comforted. She was stumbling around in a stupour, as if trying to find her way out of a strange room. Lettie thought for a moment that someone had struck her, but the poor woman's face was red and swollen from crying. She was still soundlessly weeping, an incessant stream rolling down her cheeks. She gaped confusedly at Lettie, through oddly vacant eyes.

Lettie made soothing conversation and approached warily. The sour smell of liquor floated from a wet spot on Gwenna's dress. "Come now, why not have a lie down?" Lettie chirped, guiding her towards the open study door. Gwenna muttered disconnected phrases, but allowed herself to be led, then obediently collapsed into a chaise in front of the marble fireplace of her inner sanctum.

"So sorry," Gwenna said thickly before passing out.

Lettie circled the room, pausing in front of the ornate bookcase. She methodically ran her hand across the surface. When she felt a rough area in one of the decorative scenes, she leaned down and scrutinised it, discovering a grill to an old-fashioned speaking tube. Finding the other end might prove instructive.

She next turned her attention to the japanned black writing desk, but learned nothing there; all the drawers were locked. The top of the filing cabinet was crowded with framed snapshots of Gwenna. There was also a silver framed photo of Freddie in a polo outfit, laughing into the camera. No pictures of the other men who'd once been part of Gwenna's life. There had been two husbands, Lettie recalled from the tabloid stories. Both killed in battle. Then a series of suitors, but no more marriages. And then there was Freddie. Lettie studied the mottled, inert face of the real woman, a grotesque mask in shocking contrast to the Gwenna who'd once posed for these pictures. The case had better break soon. Gwenna Hardcastle was on a rapid descent to the depths.

Lettie poked around the rest of the room, finding nothing but some interesting little capsules hidden under the false bottom of a gold-inlaid box on the liquor cabinet. She removed a couple from the unmarked envelope and rang for Bacon. Somebody would have to help carry Gwenna up to her bed.

While waiting for the butler to come, Lettie took one last look at the photos on the file cabinet. This case was unfolding like an ad for Kodak. Max's photos. The pornographic picture of Gwenna and Freddie. Montegue's party photos—so many of those! She reminded herself to give that man a call and persuade him to let her have copies.

As it turned out, Montegue proved to be most accommodating. A boy from *The Sun* delivered a box of duplicate photos to Lettie a few hours later as she and Mrs. Batney were just finishing their dinner together in one of the smaller dining rooms. Lettie was painstakingly shuffling through the photos when Julia called to report on Sam Gary. Lettie agreed that the brochure to the clinic in France sounded intriguing, might even be Hoggwell's new establishment, and said she was starting to think the doctor required watching. Julia volunteered.

"Keep me posted," Lettie said. "I'll be staying here for a few days to keep an eye on Gwenna. Poor thing isn't holding up too well."

8

GOSPORT MOTORCARS LTD. took up an entire corner of a Kensington intersection. Acutely aware of the contrast between her old banger and the chromium-plated jewels inside the showroom, Julia discreetly parked down the street.

As she walked past the plate glass, she felt like an aquarium goer gawking into a shark's picture window. Her instincts proved correct; a winking, smarmy number in a black nylon racing jacket was upon her the moment her foot crossed the threshold. He revealed a lot of bridgework and said, "Maserati!"

"I beg your pardon?"

"A new metallic amber, Connolly hides, burled elm, twin turbocharging."

"Are those magic incantations of some sort?" she asked.

"Ha ha!" The salesman laughed heartily. "That's a good one. Come have a look, Miss. The name's Taylor, by the way." He skillfully navigated her towards an undeniably sleek motorcar. "Goes a ton!" he assured, rubbing his palms together.

She looked it over, running her hand lightly along its flanks, and finally called it rather pert, an observation that discommoded old Taylor. "But a tad too—roundish. I'm looking for something more muscular."

It took Taylor but a moment to regroup and bounce back. "Ah, our Berlinetta Boxer. One previous owner, never left out in the weather, never even driven through a puddle. This way." He whisked her off to another corner of the immense show room. "Two years old. Four cams, not two!" he crooned, reverently staring down at a low-slung machine in Italian racing red.

She dispassionately regarded the flat, angular contraption that came to her knees, wondering just how someone wearing a skirt could decently get into it. "No wonder it's never been taken through a puddle—the driver would have *drowned!*" she laughed. "I'm looking for something English, and much taller."

The salesman's face momentarily slackened as he analysed his chances. Did flippant young things usually buy expensive motorcars?

"And I think I see just what I want right over there. Would you excuse me?" She walked towards Max, who was lounging in a doorway, twirling a set of keys.

Taylor retreated in defeat towards the coffee machine, muttering, "Why does *he* always get the dollies and the sheiks?"

Julia rather liked the roguish brown leather cap covering the bandage on the back of his head. It seemed a shame that such an impressive charmer wasted his time flogging cars.

"Ah, Miss Nosey-Parker! How lovely to see you again!"

"Be sweet," she warned, "or I won't tell you anything."

"Come into my office and I'll lay on the treacle," he promised, winking at Taylor, who was mooching around the front. Max closed the door behind them. "Now, what can I do for you?"

"I need someone to help me stake out a suspect. Auntie can't, she has too much on her plate at Castleberry."

"A stake out? Sounds like a Dick Francis novel."

"And you've read them all."

"I keep forgetting that you've burgled my apartment and poked into all my shameful secrets."

"Burgled!" She was properly indignant. "You found nothing missing and you know it."

"My bullwhip and Paddington Bear aren't in their customary places in my closet."

"Talk to your cleaning lady."

"Must I? She's so beneath me." He sniffed affectedly.

She looked down her nose at his sly grin. "You know, there's something slightly off about a man who wears cologne *and* a medal around his neck. Just not English, if you catch my meaning."

He laughed easily, obviously quite comfortable with his scent and jewelry. "You're absolutely right. Too body-conscious. Blame it on my Continental proclivities. But back to your original proposition—something about going out for a sirloin? Are you asking me to dinner, darling?"

"Not quite. I need someone to help me stake out Dr. Hoggwell."

"What the hell for?" For some reason he was momentarily out of snappy comebacks.

"He's putting the pressure on Gwenna to go see a psychiatrist. And making nervous noises, like he wants out of the museum project."

"So?"

"Suppose the doctor was desperate to get out, for financial reasons, say. Dirty tricks and murder could send Gwenna over the edge and give him a good excuse to queer the deal."

"All right, I'm in. I've never spied on anybody before. Who knows, I might like it."

"I expect it will be dull and nothing will happen, so don't get your hopes up."

"I have appointments until five. Let's say I pick you up at seven?"

Julia agreed and gave him her address. She left with a bounce to her step that Max and his fellow salesman watched with appreciation. "What's your secret?" Taylor asked, nudging Max in the ribs. "How do you light them up like that?"

"Continental accessories get 'em everytime."

Julia wasn't normally the sort of woman who spends hours in front of a mirror, trying to achieve just the right effect. She tended to dress for the weather and the occasion, not bothering to waste time with lengthy deliberations over what colour to wear for her complexion, whether she should show off her legs with a skirt or her bottom with a pair of trousers. Should she go for the snug sweater or the more subtle baggy shirt? But that was exactly what she'd been doing for over an hour before Max picked her up.

On her fifth outfit she suddenly became aware she was acting like a fool. In disgust, she grabbed a pair of jeans. And what if they *were* the tightest ones—they were on top, so she would wear them. Then she randomly picked a pale yellow V-necked cashmere sweater out of her drawer and pulled it over her head. She momentarily considered wearing a shirt underneath, but decided shirtless looked more casual, spontaneous. The shirt would have been too Sloanish, and she was no Sloane, so—oh gawd, she was doing it again!

She grabbed her scruffiest boots and a couple of mismatched wool socks: one red, the other purple, but who cared? That was the look she had to achieve—and the state of mind.

By the time the doorbell rang, she had made great strides towards a Zen-like state of disinterest. She shuffled over to the door, making a point of going through her mail as she let him in. "Oh, there you are. Come in while I get my coat."

But her cool was instantly blown when she looked at him. He stood there smiling at her, gorgeously casual in his own jeans and V-neck cashmere. He wasn't wearing a shirt under his either. "I was going to call you to ask what one wears on this sort of thing," he chuckled, "but it looks like I got it right."

This was too much! Her first impulse was to change clothes—no, that would be too obvious. "Just let me go put on some perfume and get a necklace, and we'll be twins," she muttered. She'd never liked that hairy-chest look before—too gigolo. But he managed to carry it off somehow.

They drove over to Belgrave Square in his Jaguar and parked across the street from the Hoggwell house.

"Here's Max on his first stake-out!" he enthused in a schoolboy gush. "You're a brick to ask me along."

"Not a-tall. Just remember that this sort of thing is like cricket—when something finally happens, one has trouble making it out."

"How will we ever pass the time?"

"Conversation might work. Tell me, how did you happen to take up gate-crashing instead of golf?"

"Actually, I *do* play golf. But the other comes more naturally. Started when I was at school, crashing other schools' parties for a lark. Then I was hooked."

"There has to be more to it than that."

"Childhood trauma, you mean? I was born with a plastic spoon in my mouth."

"I thought so," she laughed. "Do you really sell cars for a living?"

"Why not? It's easy and good money, if you've got what it takes. And I do," he modestly added.

"Well, almost" was her evil reply, as she looked around the posh neighbourhood of old established families. "Hard cheese you weren't born around here."

"Oh, I don't know. I enjoy the role: skim milk masquerading as cream."

"You ought to try for mascot status by marrying one of them."

"I almost did once," he admitted, his light tone going flat. "But her people closed ranks and she married one of the tribe. I console myself that I escaped a lifetime of starring in *Guess Who's Coming to Dinner*."

"Ah well, mustn't give up hope."

"Believe me, I haven't," he replied.

No, of course he hadn't. He was still barging their gates. Maybe next time he'd meet an orphan princess with a weakness for sports cars and hairy chests. She was beginning to dislike him again, the social-climbing cad.

"Let's change the subject," he was saying. "How did you get into snooping?"

"My Aunt Lettie," she said, dropping the brittle banter. There was nothing to be gained by it. "She's an awful meddler and always in search of material for a new plot. Lettie Winterbottom. She writes mystery novels, you know."

"Yes, I've read a few. *Death in a Stuffy Room* was fun, but not enough sex for my tastes."

"I must remember to tell her that."

There was a lengthy silence between them as they gazed at Hoggwell's front door and thought their own thoughts. Julia was acutely uncomfortable, wallowing in frustration, aware that it was all due to a wild attraction to Max that was only mildly returned. It was maddening to know that he considered her, at best, just another pretty face with no connexions. The sort who would do in a pinch, but nothing serious, thank you. She bit her lip and decided to be perfectly horrible to him every chance she got.

Max was stroking the leather cover on his steering wheel and wondering what this damned woman was really up to. Why would she want to sit all night with him in front of Tony Hoggwell's house? She must have her reasons; but he doubted if he'd ever get them out of her. She wasn't the down-to-earth, transparent sort that he preferred. Coming on to him one minute and laying on the cold, fishy stare the next. He had half a mind to call her bluff and make a pass. She'd probably pull out a service revolver and let fly. After all, she still suspected him of murder, didn't she? He stroked his hair and thought it over. No, she wouldn't be sitting here alone in his car if she were afraid of him. Or would she?

They were spared another round of verbal cat-and-mouse when Hoggwell's garage door opened and the chase was on. Hoggwell and his wife sped away in a mouse-grey Mercedes, Max's Jaguar purring along not far behind.

Hal was sitting astride a saddle in the tack room, dragging on a half-smoked fag and trying to understand what had gone wrong by studying *Kiss the Devil Good-Bye*, a Hardcastle romance set during the Age of Exploration. It was heavy going following the bilge about who was sailing where for what country, so he skipped through until he found another juicy bit. He'd just gotten to one of those (John Smith first gets Pocahontas alone) when that nosey granny walked in, bold as you please.

The old Bath Bun introduced herself and nattered something about the murder, but Hal scarcely took notice, his eyes still absorbed by the steamy encounter on the page. Smith twisted the Indian maiden's wrist and pinned her strong, writhing body against a tree. She responded by biting him on the cheek, leaving a scar he would wear for life. What did this scene have to say about the authoress, the mysterious object of his desires?

"Excuse me, Hal." Now the wrinkly old pest was shaking his book and making the words jump so that he couldn't read them.

"Leave me be," he grumbled, finally looking up at her. She was even smaller than his own Gram. Because of his grandmother, he instinctively mistrusted little women; they were always the powerful ones. It was all that power squeezed into too small a body that did it.

"Forgive me for taking you away from your book, but I'm trying to help your employer find out who murdered Freddie."

"She don't think I done it?!" Horror tore at his insides.

"No, no, but I need information from you to help catch the guilty one."

He relaxed a bit, thinking he'd better play his cards close to his chest. "What information?"

"Tell me about the job you did the night of the party."

"That was some night. I drove the big lorry over to Knightsbridge. I like being up high like that, looking down at the little bugs in their little bug cars. I could squash them just like that!" He threw back his head and howled.

The old crumpet frowned at him just like his Gram always did. They never wanted him to have any fun. "Then what did you do?"

"Brought that thing back here. They gave me some help gettin' it in the house. Not that it was so heavy, but big. Then Freddie and me had a laugh over the dummies. The woman was some popsie! Freddie said he'd grab her if he wasn't afraid of splinters. Ha ha!"

"And then what did you do?"

"Freddie said to bugger off and he let me out the back. I went to the pub and had a couple pints."

"Thank you, Hal. Gwenna will be so grateful when I tell her how helpful you've been!"

He stole another look at the old snoop. She'd called her Gwenna, like they were matey. He wished he could tell what was inside that tiny head. How much did she know about him and Gwenna? In the books they could read things in people's eyes; but he never saw anything in anybody's eyes except a little round black hole that sometimes got bigger or smaller. Maybe some people were so smart they could tell what that meant, but he wasn't.

". . . And when I tell her how you've helped me, she might not be angry with you any more." The old lady smiled and smiled, then was gone.

"Damn her!" he shouted, bounding off the saddle and impotently jumping up and down in his rage. "She's got no call to be mad, the way she's been asking for it!"

9

Rain misted across the windscreen, diffracting the streetlamps into a transparent film of golden beads. Ahead the taillamps of the Mercedes saloon held at a steady pace. Their Jaguar's motor was no more than a subdued hum, absorbed in the leather-lined cabin's cosy poshness. Only the distant bump-thump of lane markers under the treads gave any sense of movement. Julia let herself sink deeper into the seats, succumbing to the late-night fuzziness of fatigue.

Next to her Max sighed, flicked a switch, clearing the glass. "This isn't exactly a high-speed chase," he grumbled. He reached into a pocket, extracted his gold-plated case and put a cigarette to his lips, all without moving his eyes from the road.

"Life can't be all screeching tyres," she remarked, pushing in the lighter.

"Give me a life in the fast lane."

"Where do you think they're off to this time of night? Bit late to be going to a show, or visiting friends."

Max shrugged, puffing his cigarette into life. Ahead the Mercedes turned onto a main arterial, picking up speed. The traffic was slightly heavier here. "Off for a quiet weekend in the country?" he guessed, turning on the radio, tuning in the evening BBC. Mozart wafted out of the speakers. Julia could almost have fallen asleep, except for the tightness of her damned jeans. She surreptitiously reached under her sweater and undid the top button.

"Hullo!" Max leaned forward. The Mercedes, indicators winking, was taking the Dover turn-off. Max hit the brakes and tucked into the exit. The Mercedes picked up speed again. The road here was less travelled; Max dropped farther back.

"Dover?" Julia mused. "Do they intend to cross the Channel?"

He grunted and pulled out his wallet. "See how much cash I've got, will you?"

She counted his, then her own. "Together we've got sixty-five pounds."

"And some credit cards. That should be adequate."

Ninety minutes from London they were in Dover. As they trolled carefully behind, the Mercedes pulled into the British Rail long-term car park. Max cut his lights as he parked next to a truckers' cafe across the road. He rolled down his window for a better look. The odour of fish and chips immediately wafted in.

"Damn!" Julia groaned as they watched a railway porter take luggage out of Hoggwell's boot. The doctor locked his car, then followed the porter and Mrs. Hoggwell, who were entering the Dover station. There was no sign of a train as Max and Julia agitatedly pored over a schedule that he kept in his glove box. "Only two trains from here—and you can bet they're not going back to London," she said.

"It looks like our suspects are taking French leave. Very naughty. The police told us all to stay close to home until their investigations were completed. Looks like your Auntie picked the right man."

"Three large pieces of luggage seems like a lot for just a weekend jaunt."

A low rumble of diesels approached; a headlamp washed across them for a second as the train pulled into the station. Julia jumped out of the car. "Come on, we've got to get on that train before they put it on the ferry!"

Max leapt out and handed her the keys. "I'll go. You drive back to London and wait to hear from me."

Her mouth opened in surprise. "*Who* invited *whom* on this stake out? *I* will go, *you* drive back to London!"

"There's no time to argue!" he growled. He bolted across the street, Julia right behind. They ran up to the conductor as he was stepping back onto the train.

"One more, please!" Max shouted.

The conductor shook his head, saying, "This is an express," and slammed the door in their faces.

"Wait a minute! You just let someone on, we saw you!" Max yelled. The conductor shrugged as the train pulled slowly away.

"Oh charming!" Julia stamped her foot in frustration.

Max spotted the dark uniform of the night stationmaster and stalked over to complain. Julia didn't bother. What good would it do? The train was gone. She headed back towards the car, feeling very angry that they'd missed the train. And that he had tried to ditch her and continue the chase on his own. Why would he do that? Was he bored with her? Or was he one of those insufferable heroes who didn't want a woman along "to slow him down"?

He got back into the car, started up the engine. "The Hoggwells had a reservation for a sleeper from London. They gave the stationmaster a sob story about missing the train and racing it all the way here. So they are now on their way to Paris."

"There's always the hovercraft."

"Yes, I might be able to catch that."

"*I* might be able to, you mean."

He pulled away in a squeal of tyres. "Are you begging me to take you to France with me?"

"Nothing of the sort," she snapped. "*You* can stay behind."

He looked over at the set expression on her face. "I've put your back up, haven't I?"

"You're damned right! Whose bloody caper is this anyway? And where do you get off trying to leave me behind?"

"I was only thinking of your comfort. No toiletries, no change of clothes out of those tight jeans. I was being gentlemanly." It sounded good to him, but she was unimpressed.

"You were being a pig."

"Let's not stoop to name-calling so early in our relationship." He smiled winningly, but she wouldn't look at him. "It's all settled. You want to go to France with me, and I'd love to take you."

"Stuff it."

The main cabin of the hovercraft was eerily quiet as Julia and Max entered from the car hold. The overly bright strip lights shone down on polished lino, glossy enamelled steel, blue leatherette cushions. She felt decidedly shagged out; they had just spent a weary three hours waiting in the car for the last hovercraft to Calais. A few late-night denizens blinked at them as the two new arrivals sat down on a padded bench next to a window. Outside in the hoverport there was no sign of life beneath the arc lamps. Only the distant thump of withdrawing ramps gave notice that this was not some alien spaceship adrift in a cosmic fog.

"Awfully glad I decided to bring you along," he teased as the engines began to vibrate.

"I've had enough of your sense of humour for one night, thank you," she coldly replied.

"But I'm in earnest! A lonely late-night crossing would have made me morose, like that odd coot over there." He nodded at an older man in a wrinkled trench coat and beret. He had nothing but a pile of oddly wrapped parcels to keep him company. "You're a much more attractive package."

"One more irritating remark and I'll go sit with him," Julia threatened. She was past finding any of this amusing. Why did he persist in being such a lout? She vaguely stared at an amorous young couple in a corner. They were propped up against each other, sleepily whispering, pleased with themselves.

Max yawned. The murmur of engines built up to a wheezy thrum. Outside the window the quayside slowly dropped below them as the inflatable rubber skirts filled out, lifting their cabin well above the surface of the water. With a low vibration the Hovercraft left shore in a sideways scuttle.

As they gained speed, hot air poured from the vents and into their faces. Julia removed her jacket, wadded it into a pillow and stretched out on the bench. In seconds she was asleep.

Max, slouched but upright, stared into space and yawned, lost in the vibrating timelessness of late-night public transport. The few inhabitants of this glary, stuffy box looked inert, part of the fixtures. Out of time, someplace on the English Channel, between points on a map. He savoured the dislocation and watched Julia's sleeping face. His eyelids began to droop, and he leaned into a doze until his head jerked and he woke to keep from sliding out of his seat.

He went forward, pushing against the slight air blast coming from the door of the smoking deck. Outside air leaked in, overpowering the heating system. He lit a smoke, peered out into the darkness. The sea felt unusually calm beneath the deck; they would reach Calais in under an hour. But Hoggwell's ferry, while over three hours slower, had about that much head start—it would be nip and tuck. He automatically set his watch ahead an hour to Continental time.

Julia came awake at the first touch on her shoulder. She moaned, feeling muzzy-headed and momentarily unsure where she was.

"Calais in five minutes," he told her. She sat up, feeling like hell. He handed her a styro cup of hot tea. "Drink this and we'll get back in the car."

She winked the sleep out of her eyes, looked at her watch. "My God, I'm awake at half past two in the morning."

"Correction, half past three."

"Oh, right." She took an exploratory sip. "You know, this is ridiculous."

"Their coffee's even worse."

"No, I mean how can we ever race a high-speed express all the way to Paris?"

"We can't; but I'm betting the Hoggwells won't take it that far. The passenger coaches are shunted from the ferry by small yard locomotives. Then they go across the switching tracks to be hooked up to the big engines. Takes a good half-hour."

She nodded, instantly getting the picture. "A half-hour to disappear from a supposedly nonstop train." She had to admit he had his uses, the beast. "So that's why they took the train instead of their Mercedes—to confuse the trail."

"A lot of trouble for two innocent, upstanding citizens to take, wouldn't you say?"

"I would . . . if your theory is correct. You could be all wrong about this; they could be staying on until Paris."

He shrugged. "If I'm wrong, we'll have breakfast and slink home in defeat, chalking one up to experience."

The hum of the Hovercraft's motors diminished. They looked out the window to see the loading ramp lights. With a dying hiss of air, the craft settled. They stretched the kinks out of their backs and made for the stairs down to the car hold.

She longed for a toothbrush and a shower. Still, it was a lark to be travelling with nothing but the clothes on one's back and the minimal necessities in one's purse. She combed her hair as they located the dreary railroad yard.

Max found a discreet parking spot next to a small agricultural warehouse. He shut off the engine and they gave the area a quick appraisal. Locomotives, looming like houses, were ranked next to a brick and glass engine house. Repair and maintenance shops defined the treeless landscape, where only a few tufts of grass poked through the gravel.

"Do you think we've made it in time?" she wondered.

He looked at his watch, nodded. "By plenty. Let's get closer. Better leave the Jag here, though."

"Fine. It will feel good to walk."

Their shoes crunched across the gravel. An occasional bare lightbulb cast heavy shadows as they passed some anonymous corrugated building.

There was no station as such, just a loading platform piled high with produce waiting for the local goods train. A Citroën van was parked by the platform, two men in blue jumpers lounging on some vegetable crates.

The two detectives discreetly surveyed the informal car park. Julia pointed to a tarpaulin-covered object next to a pile of railroad ties. She lifted up a corner to reveal a tyre, then the front of the car. "Deux Cheveaux," Max said.

"It might belong to them," she said, indicating the railroad men.

"It might." He tried the door handle, found it locked. She produced a small pocket flash from her purse and swept it over the interior. A red Michelin guide was lying on the shelf under the dash.

"Not the sort of thing locals carry to work," she observed, extinguishing the flash. He lowered the cover and went around to the front of the car, lifting the tarp. "Someone left off the licence plates. Convenient." Looking at the twin bug-eyed headlights, he picked at a paper tag stuck onto the center of the lens, a rectangle about the size of a thumb print. "What's that?" Julia asked.

"A lamp tag. The French customs boys put them on to block out some of the beam. English lamps throw to the left. Blinds the Frenchies. Bulbs aren't yellow, either. French ones are."

"So this car is from England."

"I'd say so." He looked unshaven and tired, but suddenly cheerful. "It could be Hoggwell's getaway wheels on this side."

"Shall we let the air out of the tyres?" she suggested, catching his optimism. "But we want to see where they're going, don't we? Never mind, I'm in a fog."

"Let's get back to the Jag—I hear the train." They dashed across the street.

If it were possible to be on the edge of one's seat while being belted to a bucket seat, Julia had done it. For the last forty minutes that they had been following the Hoggwells' Deux Cheveaux, Max had insisted on not using the lights; no point in letting Hoggwell notice their English lamps, especially on these narrow country lanes.

The little French car was very slow, but this leg of the chase had still been gruelling. Max was tense and fatigued from straining to pick shapes out of the pre-dawn grey.

When there was finally enough light to see by, there was patchy ground fog to contend with. To Julia's sleep-deprived eyes, the landscape had the watery, pastel glow of an Impressionist painting: the muted golds of mown wheat fields, dull reds and greens of orchards, the startling white of a lime-coated farmhouse. Only the random dark blots of a Guernsey or Percheron appeared solid in the wavering landscape.

Far ahead the brake lights of the Hoggwells' car winked on, and disappeared to the left. They followed, turning into a narrow road lined with poplars. The thin, elegant tops of the trees vanished into the mist above. Their white polled trunks seemed to float just above the ground. Julia rolled her window down and breathed in the fresh tang of wet leaves. The damp breeze blew across her face and tangled her hair; for a moment she forgot her weariness and muscle aches and felt dreamily happy. She glanced over at Max. He turned his head towards her and smiled.

They came out of the fog, the early sunlight cutting through the mist. He automatically dropped back as the dowdy shape of the car ahead materialised. They passed a stone road marker and he slammed on the brakes. "See if you can read that *bourne*."

She stuck her head out the window and squinted at the stone. "I'll be damned!" she cried, settling back into her seat.

"What's it say?"

"Chemin du Roy. Old style spelling—it's been there awhile."

He look disappointed. "The King's Way? There must be dozens of those."

"Ah, but we're in Normandy. Drive on!" He obeyed as she added, "If we come to a river in the next few kilometres, I'll know where we are."

They crested a small rise and descended to parallel a marsh. Visibility was still poor. Around a curve they found themselves motoring along beside a broad, sluggish river. Poplars and willows grew a short way out into the water, creating miniature islands.

"Well, navigator? Where are we?"

Julia smiled. "On the Seine, of course."

"Terrific. Where on the Seine?"

"I'll give you a hint. Just look for Monet's water lilies!"

10

ON LETTIE'S SECOND DAY AT Castleberry she travelled to Brixton, from what many considered to be the most desirable part of London to the opposite end of the spectrum. Past a small grocery specialising in "Fine Kedgeree" and a tin marquee announcing the next meeting of the Sisters of the Yam, she wisped along in the dusk, trying to look straight ahead to avoid eye contact with the transients and disenchanted youth who populated the streets. Such neighbourhoods always made her aware of an intensifying wave of discontent, as if the blacks and Indians would rise up any moment for some sort of modern Cawnpoor, with a little old white lady squarely in front of the firing post.

It was with relief that she entered the door to Dr. M'Pasa's establishment. His Third World Apothecary was as eclectic as the man who was busy behind the counter. Dr. M'Pasa had begun his education in a Kenyan outdoor school and ended up graduating from Christ Church. The sight of the affable, dark, round face surrounded by a frizz of reddish-black hair never failed to bring a smile to Lettie's face. "Hello Doctor," she said.

He held up a finger, went to a file cabinet along one wall. As he leafed through notebooks, Lettie admired the mix of substances for sale: herbal medicines displayed behind little glass-paned doors jostled next to modern boxes of cold remedies. Indian health charms, an elephant-hair bracelet, a newsstand with papers in English, Hindi, and everything in between. M'Pasa played an important role in this neighbourhood, dispensing advice and guidance as much as health aides. Lettie had learned long ago that M'Pasa was certified to teach at the graduate level, but had chosen instead to work and live in a ghetto. And that was one of the reasons she had always liked him. She noticed a poster on the inside of the door that depicted a drug addict laid out on a morgue table. Written across it in M'Pasa's own handwriting was "No way out!"

"Can't be too subtle, eh Miss Winterbottom?" He was just next to her now, and his throaty growl was little more than a purr.

"Do you think it does any good?"

He shrugged. "I like to think it will stay in the back of someone's mind, make him hesitate before taking the wrong step."

"Still doing chemical analysis gratis?"

He nodded. Along with dispensing prescriptions, Dr. M'pasa would give an analysis of any substance brought in, without fee or censure. "Better they at least take an unadulterated drug than something contaminated. They know I will not lie to them." He smiled. "But I invite them to my lectures." He took out his spectacles, unfolding them as he led her into his lab in the back, saying, "But let us discuss your interesting problem." The laboratory was clean and compact, but the poor lighting from the ancient fixtures made the place resemble a sinister Dr. Frankenstein's lab. He put the folder on a table top, flipped it open. Glancing through it he said, "How long have you been bringing me these little problems?"

"Since six novels ago," she replied. It had been a lucky day when she'd attended his seminar on household poisons at a community center in Kensington, near Julia's flat. At that time Lettie had been doing research for a poisoning plot. Since then, he'd helped her a number of times.

"Well, this is one of the most dangerous drugs anyone has ever brought me. Where did you get it?"

His urgent stare alarmed her. "Why, I believe it's being prescribed by the physician of a friend of mine."

"That is impossible!"

She was completely bowled over, even allowing for M'Pasa's penchant for the boldly stated.

"I could not analyse it completely myself; but as it happens, certain large pharmaceutical firms come to me for advice. As you know, many of their greatest finds come from folk medicine. I help them with the herbs, they do a little lab work for me. And these capsules of yours," he tapped the file with a fingernail, "they contain something called Ergotathyrine II. E-II for short."

"And that is?"

"A totally prohibited, experimental compound. It is never prescribed. The company that developed it manufactures only limited quantities, for governmental research purposes only."

"What are its effects?"

"Disorientation, loss of self-protective drives. It is a thought-control drug, causing confusion, then complete submission."

"But how could my friend have gotten hold of it?" she puzzled aloud. Had Gwenna been taking it? That might explain her rapid deterioration, even the compromising photo.

"I have no idea. It is obviously against the government's interests to let a civilian get hold of a drug they use for brainwashing." He sighed, removed his glasses, and began to polish them on a lab towel. "At least that is what they called it in simpler days. Today they probably have a harmless-sounding phrase for it, like 'personality reidentification.'" He shrugged at his own joke, philosophical in the face of just one more thing he could do nothing about.

Still reeling at what she had learned, Lettie took a cab back to Castleberry. She shut herself into her room and paced back and forth in front of the hearth, trying to reason her way through the anxiety attack that was gripping her stomach. She had no proof that Hoggwell had given Gwenna those pills. Ergo, there was no reason for getting flummoxed about Julia out spying on him. Besides, Julia was a competent person. She wouldn't take foolish risks.

Bacon tapped at her door; there was a call for her. She eagerly grabbed her phone, this must be Julia now. Hearing the click of the hall extension being hung up, she said hello.

But it wasn't Julia. It was her old friend Colonel Thorn, whom she hadn't heard from since the beginning of summer. At one time Colonel Thorn and Lettie had spent a good deal of time together; but since she had rejected his marriage proposal, the dear man only called now and again. It was too bad; she enjoyed the old duffer's company, even if he was too loud and jolly for a steady diet.

"Lettie, my pet, I had the devil of a time tracking you down! I called the neighbours and they said you'd gone to visit Gwenna Hardcastle. I knew that couldn't be right. I rang Julia's but got no answer, so I decided to give it a go. What the devil are you doing there?"

"We're on a case, Colonel. So nice to hear your voice," she replied, holding the receiver far from her ear to avoid permanent hearing damage.

"I thought as much. Why else would Julia go to a salvage yard?"

"However did you know that?"

"I'm not at liberty to say." When the Colonel retired from the Army he took a job in a hush-hush governmental agency and was never at liberty to say much about anything. It was part of his problem, Lettie had decided; a man needed to talk about his work. Being a great taker of the broad hint, she had long ago learned how to glean information from his professionally sealed lips. From the vague noises he was making at the moment, she deduced that Dr. Hoggwell and Sam Gary were up to something the government considered worth watching. After a brief recital by the Colonel, she learned that the doctor had some professional connexion to a biological research company that made him privy to potentially sensitive information. This convinced her that Hoggwell was the probable supplier of Gwenna's illegal pills.

". . . And we're keeping an eye on his pal Sam Gary. There's a bloke that'd sell us down the river for scrap."

"Your man on the spot must have told you about the suspicious visitor Gary had this afternoon."

The Colonel's explosive giggle crackled across the line. "You could have knocked me over with a feather when he showed me the photograph of Julia entering the yard."

"Have you someone watching Hoggwell?"

"We do."

"I wish I had known. I wouldn't have let Julia go off to observe him."

"You didn't!"

She could just imagine his mustaches twitching in annoyance. The Colonel was very fond of Julia, often remarking that he wished her niece would settle down to marrying a decent chap and lead a normal life. He knew better than to say this to Julia, who would only make a face and a rude remark.

Lettie told him about finding the E-II and her suspicions that Hoggwell had given it to Gwenna. She could tell by the abrupt way the Colonel rang off that she was on the right track.

They stared through the windscreen at the copper plaque set into a stone column in the wall. "Le Pèlerinage." Max's tongue stumbled slightly over the *r*. "I don't suppose we should just barge in."

"Why not? Doesn't it usually work for you?" Julia chided, staring up at the pink château delineated by several tall towers that could be glimpsed behind the trees. The Hoggwells were somewhere inside.

"Oohh, aren't we testy this morning? What's the matter, luv—get up on the wrong side of the car?"

"I'm tired. And hungry. Let's go find some food."

He agreed. "Now that they've run to ground, we should be allowed a break." He pulled out into the country road, saying, "Only you've got to tell me where we are."

"Giverny, *certainement.*"

"How do you know?"

"The river, the famous road, the colours—"

"Not to mention the blinkin' water lilies. Painter country. Your old boy Monet, right?"

"You pass with flying colours. Don't tell me you're a closet art lover."

"Let's just say I've bought a few pretty postcards in my time. How far to town?"

"If we follow the river, we should be there shortly."

Later they stood next to the coupe, flexing their stiff backs and peering at the country inn. "L'Orphelin?" Max looked uninspired. "Isn't that—"

"The orphanage," Julia replied. "That's what it used to be."

"I bet that means we'll get a room the size of a closet."

"Did you say *a* room?"

"I beg your pardon?"

"Two rooms," she corrected.

"Forgive me, that's what I meant, of course."

"Good. This may be a French inn, but let's forget the French farce."

"It wouldn't be that bad, I promise you," he grinned. "But have it your way."

She turned her back on him, making a show of enjoying the architecture. The two-storied building had everything—slate roof, mullioned windows, ivy-covered chimneys.

"I hope it has modern plumbing," he muttered, rubbing his stubbled chin.

They went up the steps, past a jungle of potted geraniums, and through the door. The interior was subtly modernised. To one side of the foyer dishes clattered cheerfully from the dining room. A slim young man in tie, apron, and rolled-up shirt sleeves came out, drying his hands. He gave them a quick once-over as he went behind the desk. He handed them a pen and registration card, saying, "Everything is prepared."

"Marvelous," Max purred, accepting the card.

"You need only sign the bottom. We have the rest already filled in for your group." The man's accent was faint, his English perfect.

"So efficient!" Max beamed, showing the card to Julia. "Look, darling, they've got the old club's name in curlicues. Won't Bobby love that?"

She stared at the card. "The Lighter Than Air Society" was lettered across the top. "Super!" she bubbled. "No wonder everyone voted to come here!"

Max scribbled a signature across the bottom. The innkeeper picked it up smartly, straining to read the scrawl as he absent-mindedly referred to his typed list, which Max was already scanning upside down.

"Grendly, Harry," Max said, reading a name off the list. "I'm George's brother."

"Ah, Monsieur Grendly, I am honoured. My name is Jean Bronteau." They shook hands, Jean nodding graciously from Max to Julia.

"And this is our sister, Arabella Sloane. She left the brats with Nanny and agreed to pop along at the last moment. But it shouldn't create a problem; there are always no-shows."

The proprietor assured them that there were plenty of rooms. Keys and deposits were exchanged. Max began to build a story about their nonexistent luggage, but Jean interjected, "I understand it will be brought in the lorries? This afternoon?" They both nodded vigorously. "Very good. I understand we will have very good air!" They both heartily agreed, made their escape before they broke into giggles.

They climbed a creaking staircase that had been made for forebears less broad-shouldered than Max, who had to go up sideways. Their rooms adjoined at the end of the hall. Max was whistling cheerily as he unlocked his door. Julia followed him inside, carefully closing it behind them. "Can't resist party crashing, can you?"

He shrugged, tested the mattress with his fist, then fluffed the eiderdown at the foot of the bed. "It seemed easiest. Saved us an explanation about the luggage, arriving in the middle of the morning looking like something the cat dragged in—me not you. You look as fresh and lovely as a water lily. Must be the air!"

"I hate you," she laughed. "Just what was he talking about? Balloons? What good does this charade do us?"

"If I hadn't played along, I'd have looked like some Charlie on a dirty outing with his best friend's wife. 'A room for two and make it nippy, Belmondo. We haven't got all day!'" he snapped at an invisible clerk, then pulled her tightly against him, catching her by surprise. For a moment they just stood there, each waiting to see what the other would do. It almost took more effort than she could muster to push him away.

"Dibs on the bath," she muttered over her shoulder and made a flustered retreat towards the shower down the hall.

11

LETTIE HAD DIFFICULTY getting to sleep; she was just too worried about Julia. Over twenty-four hours and still no word, and no answer at her flat. If she hadn't had the utmost faith in Julia's abilities, she would have called the police. There was some comfort in the knowledge that one of Colonel Thorn's men would be on the scene. He would surely come to Julia's rescue if she needed him.

Lettie tossed in the grandiose four-poster and listened to a tree limb scraping against the window. This really was too large a bedroom—like trying to get to sleep in an auditorium. She longed for her cosy bedroom at home and went over the case in her mind. If only she could discover what was behind the plot against Gwenna! The key to Freddie's death would surely be there.

The problem with most of the suspects was that she just couldn't take them seriously. Mrs. Batney didn't seem the type to kill anyone; neither did Cheevers, for that matter. Even Inspector Alexander admitted that now; he'd turned him loose, in spite of witnesses' statements that Cheevers didn't get along with his employer or her phoney nephew. And then there were Penny and Hal. Pawns in the game, perhaps, but not criminal mastermind material. That left only three. Gwenna herself, a paranoid hysteric, drug addict, and possible nymphomaniac. An unstable personality that might certainly be capable of murder. Especially if Freddie had tried to blackmail her. Lettie could understand why the Inspector liked this theory. But it didn't explain the dirty tricks campaign.

Lettie yawned and once again opted for the Hoggwells and/or Sam Gary. They were up to something very nasty; she didn't doubt it for a minute. A faint sound in the hall brought Lettie to her feet. She looked at her watch—rather late for creaking floorboards and, yes, the careful latching of a door.

She hastily dressed, throwing on her fur-collared coat, and was padding swiftly down the stairs when she thought she heard the front door click shut. She crossed the ballroom and in a moment was outside, where the carriage lamps and half-moon washed the garden in blue. A dark figure bundled in a long coat was well down the drive. The elderly detective moved forward, wrapping her scarf around her neck. The air was decidedly cold. Low cirrus clouds momentarily raced across the moon.

Lettie followed her quarry a dozen blocks to an underground station. She fairly flew down the cement steps. This was more like it; something tangible was afoot.

With a distant rumble and a flutter of displaced air, the train pulled in. Lettie obtained a ticket from the automatic turnstile and, holding her scarf to her nose, went onto the platform. If anyone was looking, they'd see an old lady with a cold. Lettie took a seat in an empty carriage, near the exit so she could peek out at each stop.

The ride was long, one of the lines that went well into the suburbs. As they came out of a tunnel Lettie observed that darkness was replacing lighted streets. Soon they were past the greenbelt and racing through another suburb. To while away the time Lettie resumed her review of the case. Perhaps they were *all* up to something—

but not in concert. The idea was preposterous, although it had sold a lot of copies of *Death for Art's Sake,* her novel in which the painter of big-eyed waifs huddling in grubby alleys was jointly done in by every suspect. In real life people just weren't that cooperative; not civilians, anyway.

She wished for the hundredth time that she had met Julia at the party, as planned. Then she could have witnessed events first-hand. There was a key there, some telling detail. If only Julia would get her mind off Max Genader and back to concentrating on that night. Lettie automatically frowned when she thought of Max. A grown man who crashed parties for fun—*and* sold used cars. What kind of man was that?

At long last, near the end of the line, Lettie spotted her suspect stepping from the train. Penny Smith, the young research assistant, skittered across the empty platform and disappeared down the steps to the High Street of what was little more than a village. Lettie ghosted along after her, as evanescent and tenacious as a shadow.

Past a few blocks of shops, then the church, the post office, a row of houses. They were beyond the last of the streetlamps now, and Lettie drew closer as Penny went up a narrow dirt track. The older woman did her best to keep up, but the rough ground forced her to slow down. If Penny took a side turning, all would be lost.

After what seemed an eternity in the dark, a glimmer of white coalesced ahead. Something creaked: the dry squeal of a wooden gate. Lettie found the rustic artifact left open. A cobbled pathway meandered up to a brick wall. A heavier door was overarched by stone; set in a wall alcove stood a statue of the Virgin Mary. Lettie squinted at the carved sign above the door: "The Sisters of the Weeping Virgin."

Lettie sat down on a convenient stone bench to catch her breath and plot her next move. It was a long walk back to the station. There was nothing for it but to be bold. It was terribly rude; but there it was.

A sleepy-eyed nun quickly opened the door. "Are you in need of aid, child?" This momentarily left Lettie speechless, as she was easily twenty years the senior. Perhaps the Sister had forgotten her spectacles. Lettie put as much assertion into her voice as she could rally, considering the delicacy of her mission. "I'm so sorry to disturb you at this ungodly—I mean, inconvenient—hour, but I believe a young woman has just entered these walls. Her name is—"

"Yes, yes! Come in!" The Sister sounded crotchety. Lettie smiled as she heard her mutter something about business being brisk that night.

Lettie was ushered into a tiny chamber. She wiped the steam off her glasses with one crocheted glove while looking around the room. Rosaries and white plaster walls, pine floors smoothed by years of endless wear. A big, efficient desk piled up with papers. The Mother Superior entered, equally big and efficient. Her approach was brusque. "What is it?" She gestured towards a chair and sat behind her desk without further ado.

"I come to you on a most difficult matter."

"Yes?" A hint of asperity from the Mother Superior made her visitor smile inwardly. This was definitely a no-nonsense establishment. No martyred grins in the face of an inconvenient caller.

"It's murder, I'm afraid."

The nun looked straight into Lettie's blue eyes, trying to find the measure of the little woman who had just walked into her domain. "Sometimes . . ." she finally said, "one has a sense of a page turning over to a new chapter. This is one of those times. What do you want?" She listened to Lettie's brief explanation of the situation, then sighed. "Murder and suspicion."

"I'm sorry to disturb your tranquility with such problems."

"What is your position in this matter?"

"I'm Lettie Winterbottom. I have been asked—"

"The mystery writer? I am aware of your work," the nun said with a slight smile. "You will be discreet? Good." She settled back in her chair. "Let me tell you what I know of Penny's story."

Penny was an orphan raised by the Sisters, an order noted for its pragmatic relationship with the secular world. Aware that life in the convent hadn't appealed to Penny, the Sisters had thoroughly schooled her for the outside. Like other promising orphans she had been given an excellent grounding in literature and writing skills, history, two foreign languages, and mathematics. And, like others, Penny had been recruited.

"By Dame Gwenna Hardcastle," Mother Superior finished.

Lettie made no secret of her interest in this bit of news. "Then you have met Dame Gwenna?"

"Yes. We have been very satisfied with her over the years." She caught Lettie's quizzical look. "Oh yes, I've sent her girls for eight years now. Penny was the third."

"Each as research assistant?"

"Precisely. You won't find a better-prepared girl. Anywhere." A note of pride softened the Mother's voice. "Each worked a few years for Dame Gwenna, then went on to other positions. With a great deal more experience and a fine recommendation from their first employer."

"Where are the other girls now?"

"One has a good job with an advertising agency in Australia. The other is in the British legation in Singapore. Both positions were secured through Dame Gwenna's good offices."

"How very decent of her," Lettie murmured. This

exposed a philanthropic side of the famous author that came as a pleasant surprise. She had misjudged Gwenna, it would seem.

"She has been most charitable," the nun was saying. "And in the spirit of true charity, she requested we keep her good acts a secret. She wants no public recognition for them. I only mentioned it to you because I trust your discretion."

"I shall respect your confidence," Lettie assured her and begged her to continue.

"There is not much else to tell. It is most unfortunate that her latest protégée may not be a success. Something is distressing our poor Penny."

"So I gathered. It is imperative that she tell us the truth."

The nun's back became even straighter. "She has been taught always to tell the truth in God's house." A cloud of doubt momentarily passed over her face. "Perhaps we erred in sending her out into the world so young." Mother Superior abruptly rose and left the room.

She shortly returned with a downcast Penny Smith in tow. The girl sank into a chair while the nun sternly instructed her: "Tell us your story now, Penny. Then we will help you."

"No one can help me, not even God!" Penny replied dramatically. Her eyes were red with tears.

"You must never say that," the nun admonished. "God always helps us."

"Not me, I'm a murderer. I killed Freddie."

Her audience stared in dumb shock until Lettie found voice to ask why.

"I loved him. I thought he loved me. When I found out he was just using me, I went insane." She pitifully looked to the nun for sympathy, sobs shaking her shoulders.

"There's no time for tears now," the Mother Superior gruffly said.

Penny obediently took a deep breath and wiped her eyes on her sleeve. "He said we'd run away together. Just as soon as he got his money. What a fool I was to believe him!" Freddie apparently had promised Penny a romantic escape in exchange for her helping him wage war on Gwenna. "Somebody was going to pay him several thousand pounds if he could drive Gwenna mad. That was the original plan." She insisted she had no idea who was behind it all or what the purpose was. "I didn't care. I hated Gwenna and loved Freddie. It suited me just fine to go along with it."

It had started out as an amusing game; they'd meet secretly and see who could come up with the best trick. The guest list had been Freddie's idea. "We laughed and laughed over that one. She's such a snob, you know. Those parties were like the Queen's coronation." Penny didn't bother to hide her resentment. "My best idea was the love letters. I wrote long, steamy notes and signed them with Gwenna's initials. Then Freddie would leave them in Hal's room over the stables. Freddie got impatient, though, didn't think they were enough to get Hal to act. So he started dropping hints to the little dimwit, goading him on. He would give Hal some brotherly advice on how to make his move. She was there for the taking, Freddie said, Hal had only to play his cards right and he'd have himself a rich old wife. Hal's an idiot, you know. It wasn't hard to convince him." Penny shook her head and laughed humourlessly.

"That explains Hal's attack on Gwenna."

"Yes. Too bad it came after Freddie was dead. He would have enjoyed it so." She started to laugh again, but swallowed it in the face of the nun's disapproving look.

Worried the nun might glare the girl into silence,

Lettie encouraged her to continue the story. The detective was anxious for the next revelation.

The war had been going nicely until about a week before the party, when Freddy started getting impatient. He told Penny it was high time they got paid, but the money man seemed to want more from them. "Freddie was livid, said he couldn't wait for us to be living together on our Greek island in the sun. He was good at that—telling a girl just what she wanted to hear." There were several minutes of pregnant silence. So much for life on the outside, Lettie mused, guessing the nun was thinking along similar lines. "That's when he made up his mind to blackmail Gwenna and get out. I offered to help, of course. I thought he was going to use some information I'd given him, but I found out the night of the party that he had something even better . . ."

Lettie's ears perked up. "What information had you given him?"

"I can't tell you!" Penny shouted at Lettie. She glanced at the nun and lowered her voice. "I'm sorry, Mother." Then she turned to explain to Lettie, "I admit that I hate Gwenna Hardcastle—but I owe her something, after all the shameful things I've done." She said that Freddie's original plan had been to confront Gwenna after the party, when she'd be exhausted and upset by all the uninvited guests. He was going to demand ten thousand pounds for not telling what he knew to the press." The girl had mastered her emotions, now telling the rest so matter-of-factly that it sent a chill down Lettie's spine as she fathomed the depths of Penny's hatred for Gwenna and the man who had misused the girl's affections.

As soon as the party was under way Penny had gone out onto the balcony to enjoy Gwenna's reaction to the unwanted guests. But what she wound up watching was her own true love in action. "Kissing and pawing every female he could get his hands on. Then I knew that he didn't give a damn about me. It had all been a lie."

"What did you do?"

"Nothing for a while. It was funny, I couldn't move. And I actually saw red, which I'd always thought was just a figure of speech. The whole scene was suddenly washed in red, like somebody'd turned on a red spotlight. There was Freddie with his arms around two women, laughing and having a grand old time. That's when I knew I was going to kill him."

"My dear child!" Mother Superior cried, breaking her judicious silence. She clasped Penny's hands in hers, which produced the opposite of the calming effect intended.

"Don't interrupt me, please," the girl begged, pulling her hands away. "Or I won't be able to tell it."

Penny said she knew she had at least a half-hour before Freddie would break into Gwenna's study. It was part of his plan to make her especially paranoid that night. Too agitated just to wait, she went and searched his room. "I'm not sure I knew it at the time, but I wanted to know every terrible thing I could about him, to fuel my anger. I found some IOU's that added up to quite a sum. He must have been into a loan shark or bookie, someone named O'Hara. That wasn't much of a surprise; I knew he liked the horses. What really rocked me was one document proving he wasn't Freddie Hardcastle at all, but someone named Brian Fogelstock. And there was a photograph of him and Gwenna. I almost threw up when I saw it."

"Then you knew what he intended to use for blackmail," Lettie supplied.

"Yes, then I knew. I took the evidence back to my room and hid it. Then I watched the downstairs corridor. When he went back down the hall, I slipped down the stairs and followed him." She shuddered, reliving the scene. "I found him drinking in the study. I called him a monster, told him he wasn't fit to live. He just laughed and said something very cruel. Then I hit him."

Lettie leaned forward in her chair and tensely asked, "With what?"

"The whiskey decanter. It didn't even chip. That's good crystal for you." Penny's eyes were far away. "He just lay there," she whispered. "I knew he was dead. I wiped off the decanter, ran upstairs, and locked my door."

Mother Superior regarded the sinner with genuine compassion, while Lettie could only feel frustrated impatience at the moment. If this was all there was to the girl's story, Penny had nothing to worry about. "Did you hear anyone come up the stairs or go past your room at any time?"

Penny hadn't. She'd wanted to go back to see if he was really dead, but was afraid. Later she heard drums and went back out onto the balcony to see what was happening. A spotlight was on the diorama and somebody was screaming "Murder!" She'd later heard about the sword. "I don't know how that happened, or who put him in the diorama. I left him lying on the floor of the study."

Lettie told her she was a very lucky girl. "The autopsy showed the sword killed him—not the blow on the head."

"Me, lucky?" The strident rattle of a laugh again. "So they won't hang me after all? But I was beginning to look forward to it."

This melodramatic declaration was too much for the nun. She made a stern remark or two that brought a properly chastened look to Penny's face.

"Why didn't you tell the police?" Lettie wanted to know.

"I was afraid—mostly of Hardcastle. I just couldn't face her . . . I'm an awful coward."

"Not any more," Lettie said briskly. "You're going to speak up and help catch the real killer. Now try to remember, you passed the diorama on your way into the study."

"But I didn't even look at it. I was too caught up in having it out with Freddie."

"How did the library look?"

Penny frowned in concentration. "It was a mess. The furniture was pushed against the window, the rug moved to one side. The diorama filled most of the room. Even though it was against the wall, I remember I had to squeeze past it to get to the study."

"So there was little room to move. Think of how it was all arranged—was there a place in the library where someone could have been hiding?"

"The one who stabbed him, you mean? There all the time listening to Freddie and me?" The girl paled; this cast a horrible new light on an already awful memory. She closed her eyes and put herself back in the library. "No, you must be mistaken. The furniture was so tightly against the window there was no room for someone to be hiding behind it. The curtains were too short to conceal a person—and they were open."

"And the diorama?"

Penny made a confused gesture. "I don't recall. I hardly looked at it. But I certainly didn't see someone just standing in it."

Lettie sat back and tried to relax, suddenly aware of how tense her neck muscles had become. There was no use trying to force a memory that wasn't there. She tried a different tack. "What about later, when you looked down from the balcony? What could you see of the scene then?"

"Not that much."

Abandoning what seemed to be a blind alley, Lettie asked her to recall that last painful encounter with Freddie. "Did you get the impression he was still intending to follow his schedule and threaten Gwenna with blackmail *after* the party?"

Penny looked confused. "I don't know. What are you getting at?"

"Did he say anything to indicate that he intended to meet her then—after he got rid of you? Or that he'd already confronted her earlier?" It was a vital point for or against Gwenna.

Comprehension dawned. "Oh, I see! You think Gwenna came in after me and stabbed him to death when he tried to blackmail her!" This new possibility brought the colour to Penny's pale cheeks. It was a solution that appealed to her sense of justice. She wanted it to be true. Her face fell as she thought of a problem. "But how could he? I'd taken the photograph by then."

"He might have had a copy he was carrying with him. Or perhaps he just started softening her up with your lesser bit of blackmail first."

Penny nodded. Hope returned. "If she didn't kill him, she should have!"

The nun looked suddenly very tired as she contemplated one of her worst failures. After a good night's sleep she'd begin work setting this one straight. Tonight it was impossible even to hope.

Lettie too was weary, but had to pursue this last point. "But did Freddie give you the impression that he expected anyone to meet him there?"

Penny had to admit he hadn't. And, as much as she hoped it were true, she had no reason to believe he'd changed his plan to blackmail Gwenna after the party.

"Just one more thing and I'll be on my way," Lettie said. "I assume you sent the documents and photo to the police?"

Penny had. "I wanted the truth to come out about them. The whole disgusting truth."

12

JULIA DREW THE BEDCLOTHES closer around her, clinging to them like the last wisps of a dream. She was precariously curled near the edge of the lumpy mattress to avoid the depression in the middle. The dream evaporated as the realities of a new day intruded with a bang. She moaned and reached for the clock, but there was none. She groggily sat up, wondering if the rhythmic thunder was coming from under the floorboards or inside her own head.

She put bare feet on the cold floor, felt the thudding stop after a moment. She reached for a robe, then remembered she didn't have one. No pajamas either; and the room was distinctly chilly. She padded across the floor and hurriedly pulled on her clothes, the ones it seemed she'd been wearing for weeks, but actually for only a day. There were no clothing shops in the village—she'd looked yesterday afternoon while Max was ingratiating himself with the Lighter Than Air Society, which involved doing a lot of steady drinking and talking. She didn't like this latest persona of his—the spoiled English bore on a pub crawl. She had avoided him and the whole ghastly crowd, escaping to wander through Monet's wonderful garden, now all but over for this year.

By evening she had no choice but to return to the inn and have too many "snorts and wets." Their jokes were nauseatingly puerile, with Max telling as many as anyone. He fit in so well it made her want to "park a custard," a key phrase in the lexicon of Max's new pals. She had been reluctantly impressed by his ability to assume the natural colouration of his environment.

The vibration beneath her feet started again, and she decided it was the hammering of ancient plumbing. There would be a line for the bath down the hall. At that moment there came a light tapping at her door.

"Go away," she said.

"Never," came Max's cheerful call through the panel. "Get a move on, it's going to be a wizard day."

"Oh, God. What time is it?"

"Five A.M., sweet slug-a-bed. Get up!"

She threw open her door and glared at him. He smiled idiotically as she yanked him in by the arm and slammed the door behind him. Once inside, his face resumed its normal intelligent look. "If you don't drop that moronic act, I'm going to strangle you," she warned between clenched teeth.

"Come on, get into the part, darling. We must blend in with the crowd, mustn't we?"

"You're blending in too well. Your jaw's starting to recede; another day and you'll be a complete twit."

He looked worried. "You think I'm laying it on a tad thick?"

"Definitely."

He was properly chastened. "I'll play it straighter."

"Please."

He gave her an oddly warm look. "You're a tough critic, aren't you? Please remember this is my first detective caper." His face split into an engaging grin. "You're a hard woman to please."

"And don't you forget it." She leaned back, folding her arms across her chest.

He threw back his head and laughed, his real, wonderful one, not the idiotic giggle he'd been affecting. She laughed too, but he cut it short by saying, "Get your arse in gear. We're going up in half an hour."

"What?"

He walked out without elaborating.

From green boots they called "Wellies" to funny ponycart caps, they exuded not just Britishness but the smug jocularity of the City, specifically SW1, the headquarters of the upper-class creatures recently dubbed Sloane Rangers, after their native Sloane Square. Their noisy chatter and scrubbed outdoorsiness exuded the joy of being The Right People. Most of them sported awful black, waxy jackets bulging with pockets and smelling of dog. Inwardly cringing at their sophomoric banter, Julia went along for the ride.

They were bucketing along a dirt track in a Range Rover, a complete hot air balloon packed away on the roof. Julia was scrunched between Max and an obnoxious boy called Winnie, who stank of Ralph Lauren cologne, sweat, and Golden Retriever. Winnie nattered on and on, but Julia found most of his jargon incomprehensible. Max made an occasional exclamation in the right places, all the while navigating from a map on his knee and a pencil flash in hand, shouting out instructions to Andy, who was behind the wheel.

Their driver had a pronounced tendency to devote equal attention to his "babylegs" girlfriend, plastered next to him, in short skirt and pastel tights, and the demands of predawn driving. They all screamed when Andy nearly hit a tree in the middle of a lingering embrace. It even scared Babylegs, who finally took her hands off him long enough to light a cigarette to a general cry of "Defug! Defug!" Windows were rolled down as cackles filled the cabin.

"We're going to be killed," Julia muttered in Max's ear.

"Yes, but it will be worth it, I promise," he murmured back, his warm breath tickling her ear. "Mind if I nibble your ear? My breakfast soggies didn't satisfy."

She gave him her best sneer in reply.

"Hey, what does a Frenchie do first thing in the morning?" Max called out to the general crowd, pressing his thigh against hers. She looked away, plotting revenge.

Mercifully for Julia, the Range Rover soon fishtailed to a halt at the end of a dirt road. She eagerly got out, seriously considering taking off across the meadow and back to the inn. But Max took her to one side, explaining in hushed tones, "Here's the gen. We're directly upwind from Le Pèlerinage. I did a little mapwork last night. We'll need a bit of time to float there, since there isn't much breeze and these babies are difficult to launch; but we should be over our destination by the time the sun comes up. A little aerial reccie before lunch, if we're lucky!"

A Volvo wagon pulled up beside the Range Rover and disgorged a fresh crew of Sloanes keen to work.

"More?" Julia groaned.

"We need all the help we can get. There's no time to twitch your nose—we've got to get airborne!"

Boots crunched over the stubble of mown flax, the first hints of dawn just picking out the light dusting of frost on the earth. Under the glare of the Volvo's lights, the Rover was off-loaded. Julia shivered and watched them bray at each other, acting and looking alike in their Huskies, Barbours, and baggy cords.

"Come on, whiz!"

"Toss that over!"

"Do kick on, Caroline, the sun's coming up!"

They tossed equipment about and spread out the immense nylon envelope with the enthusiasm of young pups, never standing still. A tribe, Max had called them— a tribe of ninnies, Julia thought.

She tried to engross herself in the details of preparing for ascent. The main body of the balloon stretched out a good hundred feet, including the lines. Max was helping to clip them to the gondola, which to Julia's eye resembled a glorified laundry hamper. Above the basket, still turned on its side, was a mish-mash of pipes and gas bottles that looked like a Victorian hot-water heater. Two men were stooped over this, making sparks with a flint lighter while bemoaning the results of the night before. "I've got a senior hangover." "I'm feeling a bit silly myself."

"Hog whimpering," someone else chimed in. With a loud pop the hissing gas ignited into a fluttering blue flame. Senior Hangover turned a knob, the flame lengthened, lightened into a blue corona around the mouth of the burner. Gusts of hot air blasted out as the two manoeuvred the unit towards the open collar of the balloon. A third party lifted up the fabric, allowing the superheated air to blow in. Within minutes the fabric began to swell, billowing up in loose lumps. Someone disappeared inside, shaking out the envelope as it filled and became a wobbly spheroid.

With practised coordination, others in the crew manned their tethers as the bag gained buoyancy, struggling up into the air like a rising custard.

It was not long before it floated over them, round and without a wrinkle. The gondola, upright now, bobbed in readiness. Julia stamped her feet against the cold and rather liked the look of it. The panels were done in alternating gores of red and blue that shone silkily in the first rays of sun peeking over the nearby ridge. It had all the simplicity and beauty of a child's drawing.

Andy, as pilot, completed his inspection of the equipment, and rations were loaded on board. Cello bags full of fresh loaves and cheeses were thrown in, a silver flask or two stashed into pockets. Andy stepped in, then Babylegs, Max, and a reluctant Julia. Once aboard, Julia realised, to her horror, that the gondola barely came past her waist. Even being a few inches off the ground inspired nauseating fear. She positioned herself in a corner, fighting an impulse to curl up into a foetal position as Andy and Babylegs pawed each other excitedly. The little door was latched, the map consulted one last time. Despite her borrowed husky, Julia felt shivers run down her spine—fine time to remember her fear of heights. "Will it be colder up there?" she managed to ask in an even voice.

Andy broke free from his clinch and shook his head. "We'll be whizzing along at the same speed as any breeze we can pick up," their pilot explained, then began pointing out the salient controls to an eager Max. "Now this is the throttle, you could say." He tugged on an overhead cord, eliciting a dragon's roar from the burner, which was now a few feet over their heads. "More heat, more height." He gestured to the bags of sand dangling from the side of the gondola. "And ballast to be used as needed. No bombing runs on the natives, no matter how tempting."

"Check. And to come down?" Max asked.

"We can let the bag cool down. Or, if we're in a hurry, there's that." He indicated a red handle that was locked with a pin. "Opens up the top of the bag—takes you down in a rush. Not recommended over a hundred feet or so. Everyone set?" Babylegs giggled expectantly, Max and Julia nodded.

The throttle was yanked and held down, the burner

roared as the tethers were released. The thin floor creaked and moved beneath their feet, almost like the motion of a small boat cresting a wave. Only this boat continued to rise at what felt to Julia like a terrifying speed. Her hands locked on the rim of the basket that measured a mere five feet on a side. Her knees jellied. They were already well above the stand of poplars that bordered the field. And she could see into the next, as hedgerows began to spread out below.

The burner roared on; the river appeared in the distance, a rambling sheet of glossy material. They ascended out of the shadow of the hill and into sunlight that was surprisingly warm. They could look down now on the crest of the hills below and behind them. Across the valley the dark line of the opposite hills emerged from the gloom. With a sudden, gut-wrenching silence the burners stopped, and Julia instinctively tensed a bit more. Andy's conversational volume seemed to boom out of the hush. "Five thousand, near as I can figure."

"A mile!" Julia gulped. Straight up. With perhaps an inch of creaking basketry between them and the ground! But she couldn't help smiling.

Because it was quiet. Not just the buzzing emptiness of an insulated room, but the cathedral silence of great and open space. They were floating in a great dome of air. Pacing the wind in their noiseless contraption, they floated in their own bubble above a delicate landscape: the metallic threads of streams feeding into a marsh, patchwork fields, a curl of smoke from a farmhouse. After a few moments of this remarkable silence, an occasional sound, ethereal and distant, rose up to them. The clap of a back door slamming, the fraternal salutations of ducks in the marsh. A cock's crow, the squeak of a cable over their heads. Entranced, Julia relaxed and released her death grip on the basket. "Marvelous!" she breathed as Max moved closer and flashed her a look that said,

"Isn't it lovely to be alive?" She beamed back, for once in agreement with him.

Fortunately Andy turned out to be a better pilot of balloons than Range Rovers. He remained at the controls, studying his barometric altimeter between nuzzlings of Babylegs's blonde hair.

The moving shadow line was distorted by the pebbly texture of the fields as the sun steadily climbed. Once in a while the burner would rumble on for a few seconds, stabilising their altitude.

Max produced a hip flask and passed it round. Julia took a sip of Cherry Heering and whiskey, the first drink she had ever had at sunrise.

Max drew her attention to the pink château coming into view. "Look familiar?" It was a spawling establishment with an odd array of towers distinctive even at this distance.

"Le Pèlerinage."

"Mmm-hmm. Let's hope the Hoggwells are still at home."

"This *is* a wonderful way to case the grounds," she had to admit. He looked pleased that he had managed to impress her.

The house was situated in the center of a green stretch of cultivated acreage: orchards between the country road to the front and vineyards to the rear. Immediately behind the house was a scattering of cottages rimming a large parking area. In spite of the well-tended grounds, the place had a recently abandoned air about it, as if everyone had left for the season. There were no cars to be seen, no one stirring.

Their progress was painfully slow in terms of aeronautical devices, but every time Julia looked away to enjoy the view, she found that the pink château had grown larger.

Max had a chummy conversation with their pilot,

who regularly consulted his watch or the altimeter. He even crumpled up a pastry wrapper and dropped it over the side, intently watching its fall and trying to judge their true ground speed. He finally nodded and Max clapped him on the arm.

Max returned to Julia's side and leaned casually on the edge of the gondola, making it bulge out alarmingly. "About ten minutes," he said. "We're going down now."

"Just what do you have in mind—bombing the doctor with dead soldiers?" She nodded towards Babylegs, who was tipping an empty champagne bottle over the side.

"Just a little reconnoitreing; our shadow's behind us and they certainly won't hear us coming."

"So this is why you were kissing up to them last night. I thought you were doing it for fun."

"That too, of course. But mostly for you, darling. See how I put myself out for your funny little case?"

"Above and beyond the call of duty."

"At least a mile."

Deprived of its source of internal combustion, the balloon rapidly lost its lift. They were soon under a thousand feet. Julia was glad to see the ground getting closer.

As they drifted nearer to the rosy painted towers, the partially denuded limbs of the trees beckoned. "Need a tiny bit of altitude," Andy said, reaching for the burner's rope.

"Don't be so wet." Max draped a casual hand on their pilot's arm. They were little more than a hundred feet up now.

Julia looked for Hoggwell's car in the drive as the balloon crept down over the central gravelled area behind the main house. The only vehicle in the open was a blue delivery van at the back of the house. They got a quick glimpse of a flagstone patio between what appeared to be two guest cottages. A woman in a dressing gown was sitting at a wrought iron table and reading a newspaper.

"Andy, don't!" Babylegs mildly protested. Julia looked to see him about to drop one of his shoes over the side.

"Bung ho!" he yelled. The newspaper reader jerked to attention, looked from side to side, then behind her. She got up and disappeared inside the cottage.

Whether Andy would have dropped the other shoe would never be known, for at that moment the gondola lurched downward like a runaway lift in a skyscraper. Julia thought she saw Max's hand pulling the red handle as they crashed into the courtyard, narrowly missing a cottage.

The basket hit and bounced, spilling them out as the deflating bag dragged the gondola across the gravel. The balloon, freed of its passenger load, struggled for one last moment, rising just enough to catch itself on a corner tower. Like a child's toy with its last bit of air leaking out, it draped itself elegantly over the side of the old, vine-covered walls of the house.

Spitting out a faceful of gravel, Julia got to her feet and confronted Max, who was hurriedly dusting himself off. "You maniac!" she sputtered.

"Spang on!" Max proudly declared. "Not bad for an amateur navigator, if I do say so myself." He grabbed her hand, dragging her away from their fellow passengers, who were unhurt and giggling in a tangled pile on the ground.

"What now?" Julia hissed.

"Snoop around, obviously."

He made a beeline for the back of the mansion, but Julia balked. Ignoring his emphatic motions to follow, she dashed back across the gravel to the scene of the crash. She wanted to have a look at those guest cottages, and the woman with the newspaper. Andy was balefully examining the dented flask he claimed had mashed his pelvis. Babylegs hastily stuffed her contraceptives back into her handbag, as someone in his shirtsleeves came dashing towards them from the house. Julia avoided the scene by ducking under the arbor between the cottages. The patio was now empty, the newspaper dropped on the stones, a pair of glasses left on the table.

She looked around. The patio was a charming private retreat in the sun. A few bees sleepily buzzed among the last marguerites of the season. The walls of the buildings were a faded pink stucco, like the main house. The windows were trimmed in thin strips of chalky blue. The shutters on both cottages were drawn from the inside; but Julia noticed a flicker of movement behind one of them.

These were too spruce to be workers' residences. She wondered who the woman on the patio had been. A weekend visitor? Was this some sort of resort? Only one way to find out.

Julia knocked at the door and, getting no response, tried the latch. It was unlocked, so she went in. The room was decorated with country simplicity—bare wood floors, whitewashed walls relieved by a few alcoves housing flowers and books. Old but good furniture arranged around a low coffee table. She picked up one of the magazines: *Country Life*. The others were English too: *The Tatler, Horse and Hound,* a recent Christie's catalogue.

There didn't seem to be anyone about, so she went into the tiny kitchen. There were a few jars of jam and packets of tea on the shelf, next to biscuits and some tinned soup. The fridge was almost bare: a wedge of cheese, a bowl of eggs, apples in the crisper. Behind her someone moved. Blushing guiltily, Julia whirled around to encounter Benecia Hoggwell in a dressing gown about to slip from her bony shoulders. Her eyes were large and vague, her cheeks very pale. "Haven't we met? Are you the therapist?" she asked the intruder.

"Not exactly. Am I disturbing your breakfast?" Julia heard herself saying, though she didn't know why. Maybe because the woman really looked starved to death.

"You *are* the therapist! Didn't they tell you that I can't keep anything in my stomach before noon?" Benecia's eyes glistened with tears.

Stunned, Julia watched her crumple to the floor, and in a flash guessed what brought the Hoggwells to Le Pè lerinage. Recalling the night of the party, Julia now understood why Mrs. Hoggwell had looked so ill in the powder room. She must have eaten some hors d'oeuvres, then purged them away right before Julia had walked in. Purge—a nice, sanitary word. Julia recalled an article she'd read about anorexia and bulimia. If left untreated, these disorders could lead to serious complications, even damage a victim's heart.

"Where is your husband?" Julia asked, helping Benecia to her feet.

"I expect him in a few days at the latest. He had some other things to take care of while we're here."

There were any number of questions Julia would have liked to ask, but she sensed the woman's meager strength had already dissipated. She encouraged her to rest, and couldn't resist trying to press some food on her. "I'd be glad to make you some eggs."

Benecia refused, saying the nurse would be bringing a special protein drink to her soon. "Then she'll watch me, to make certain I keep it down." She said it playfully, a naughty child confessing to a bad habit.

"You want to stay alive, don't you?" Julia asked, well aware that it must be a great deal more complicated than that in Benecia's mind.

"That's what Tony always asks," was the evasive reply.

Disturbed, but unable to think of anything else to say, Julia left in search of Max.

13

Lettie was sipping tea in Inspector Alexander's office when he came in at eight on the fourth morning of her investigation. There was a white blob of shaving cream beside his ear. He had the distracted air of one not yet prepared to face another workday. Lettie, on the other hand, in spite of getting little sleep after the previous night's chase to the nunnery, was still alert and keen to get on with it. She felt that a break in the case was at hand, and the excitement gave her plenty of energy.

She detailed Penny's confession while the Inspector ravaged his tea and buns. He perked up at the part about the blackmail, latching onto it as an excellent motive for Gwenna to kill Freddie, just as Lettie knew he would. It would be damned difficult to prove, of course. "But that's the way this case is going," he sighed. "I had to let Cheevers go yesterday because there just wasn't enough to hold him."

She said she was glad and inquired if he'd given any thought to inheritance as a motive for murder. Kill Freddie off, drive Gwenna to suicide—or kill her and make it look that way.

The Inspector said there was no one who stood to inherit a great deal. Most of Gwenna's fortune would go to a nunnery, except for the sizable amount earmarked in case the museum didn't show a profit. He intimated that her estate could support it for a hundred years.

"A memorial to herself. Oh well, she won't be the first—or the last."

He said Lettie was a treasure for being on the spot—otherwise a couple of his men might have wasted a day or two tracking Penny down. He blotted his mouth with a handkerchief and grabbed the phone, ordering a couple of men out to the nunnery to pick up the research assistant.

"You will charge her, then?"

"Not at the moment. Let's wait and see how her story agrees with the evidence."

"I, for one, believe she was telling the truth—as far as she went."

"Or else she's clever enough to confess her lesser crime: 'I hit him, but I never ran him through!'" The policeman slapped his thigh and stood up. "Come along, I'll give you a ride back to Castleberry. I've suddenly got an uncontrollable urge to paw through Miss Smith's personal effects. Might see something I missed the first time."

Penny's room was a combination bedroom and office done up in pink and green Laura Ashley wallpaper and thick green carpet. The landscape paintings and ceramic knick-knacks somehow contributed to the room's lack of personality. It was not hard to imagine a young woman working here—papers were piled all over the big library table. But the room had none of the personal paraphernalia one expected to find in a young person's room.

The Inspector concentrated on the desk while Lettie floated around, pausing in front of the ornate scenes that decorated the built-in bookcases on either side of the fireplace. Her eye immediately focused on a familiar motif.

She bent over to examine it and heard a distinct but microscopic cough.

Intrigued, Lettie looked over her shoulder; her companion was a good thirty feet away. It hadn't been he. And there was no one else in the room.

She leaned down and took a look at the interior of a trumpet flower in the design. Behind the latticework of carved vines, she could make out a cleverly disguised joint. She put her ear to it and heard a faint roar, like one heard in a sea shell. She inserted her finger and pulled; the entire flower swivelled out on brass hinges. A leather plug came with it, shrunken by years of dry heat from the fireplace.

"Inspector!" she called, after putting her hand over the circular opening that had been revealed. She pointed at it, a finger to her lips.

Alexander looked it over, then carefully closed it up. He took her across the room before saying a word. "Old fashioned speaking tube."

"And there was someone at the other end—I heard a cough."

He rubbed his chin. "I'd better go find out who is on that other end—wherever it is—while you take a look at this." He indicated a thick sheaf of papers bound together with brads.

"It looks like a manuscript."

"And it wasn't here last time I went over this room. See what you make of it 'til I get back. It might be a while—forty rooms makes things difficult."

"Oh, I already know where the other end comes out!" She smiled, relishing his amazed look. "And who is on the other end."

"Speak up, woman! Don't drag it out like a clue in a mystery novel!"

She chuckled quietly. "Forgive me, Inspector. I believe I can safely wager that I heard Gwenna Hardcastle at her writing desk. When I was in her study I noticed an identical flower designed into her bookcase."

The Inspector made appreciative noises that she modestly brushed aside, turning her attention to the hand-written manuscript entitled "Ghostly Passion." There was no author's name on the title page. "Inspector, could you find me a sample of Penny's hand?"

He quickly located a note signed by the research assistant. Even to an untrained eye, the similarities were apparent. "Not much doubt she wrote both," he observed.

Lettie studied the first chapter. It was another reworking of the old Cinderella story, about a poor, exploited ghostwriter who falls in love with her cruel employer's handsome son.

Putting two and two together, Lettie pulled a couple of recently published Hardcastle novels from the shelf and compared their sentence structure and phraseology to the manuscript's. After a while she looked up at him with a triumphant gleam in her eyes. "Penny is the author of these particular Hardcastle novels. I'd stake my reputation on it!" It fit perfectly with the pattern: young girls without families or confidants, sequestered for years while they wrote their own romantic fantasies to the Hardcastle formula. Then at the first glimmer of independence, shipped off to a desirable new position in some far-off spot—Rangoon or the Antipodes. So this was what Penny had refused to tell the night before. Lettie wondered why. Out of some small sympathy for Gwenna?

The policeman looked fascinated, but uncomfortable. "Dame Gwenna would string my guts in the breeze if any of this came out." He paced around the desk, fretting. "But I've got to confront her with it."

"I will, if you like," she offered; and the reluctant

policeman readily accepted, remarking he'd listen in over the speaking tube.

She passed Bacon on her way to the study. "Madame must not be disturbed while at work," the butler dutifully cautioned.

"Thank you, but I doubt that she's writing." Lettie breezed past; and Bacon, knowing an irresistible force when he saw one, made no move to stop her. She tapped briskly on the study door. There was no reply. She tapped harder and called out, "It's vital that we talk!"

"Not now," came the muffled response.

"It's urgent! Penny's run away!"

"What?" The door was flung open and a panicky Gwenna breathed liquor in Lettie's face. It was before noon—rather early for brandy. But she did look in better shape than the day before. Lettie glanced at the box that hid the pills and wondered about the best way to handle that problem. She decided to steal them.

Lettie pushed into the room. The writing desk was clear. The only work in progress was drinking. She turned to Gwenna, who was unsteadily sinking into her chaise and moaning, "Not Penny, no, not Penny!" She fell heavily back against the cushions and stared up at the harbinger of bad news, a mixture of fear and entreaty quivering her red lips.

"It's true. She ran away last night."

"Oh my God! You must find her!" the distraught woman cried, grasping for her brandy glass.

"I already have."

"Thank God!" Paranoia replaced relief as she took a long drink. "Where?"

"At the convent. I know everything." Lettie informed her.

She couldn't meet Lettie's eyes. "I don't know what you mean."

"I know about your ghostwriters," Lettie said softly.

At first the Queen of Historical Romance continued to feign bewilderment. Ghostwriters? Whatever gave Lettie that absurd idea? But when Lettie pointed to the speaking tube in the bookcase and showed her the manuscript of "Ghostly Passion," Gwenna's indignant facade crumbled into a whining tirade. What was wrong with ghosts? Lots of famous writers used them. There was certainly no law against it. "After all, it's the Hardcastle name that sells books, not the contents. Penny's just a nobody. She'd never make a living writing under her own name."

"Perhaps not at first," Lettie admitted. "But given the chance, she might build up a name for herself."

"Hardly likely," Gwenna sniffed. "She's much better off with me. I'm paying her a salary. And if she'd worked here for three years, I'd have given her a bonus and found her other employment."

"Some place far away from England and your fans. Or should I say *her* fans?" Lettie's sad expression somewhat softened her words, but Hardcastle was accepting no blame.

"How dare you be so self-righteous! My eyes are bad. I've suffered from writer's block for fifteen years. Can you cast that up to me? One's libido wants to retire when you get as old as I am. And the libido is where my kind of art comes from." Indignation had faded into embarrassment; she had never admitted anything so damning to anybody. "Surely you can understand that?"

"What I can't understand is your treatment of the girl," Lettie answered. "Penning her up like a prisoner, treating her rudely. You taught her to despise you."

"I treat my servants like servants, not like friends."

"And what about Freddie—how did you treat him?"

"Like the son I never had." Bitter, beaten words.

"Then I am truly sorry for you," Lettie said feelingly.

"Did he demand hush money the night of his death? Blackmail to keep quiet about your ghostwriter?"

Gwenna looked stricken at this second blow. "I don't know what you're talking about."

"It's a fine motive for murder."

"That's insane! No one was blackmailing me!"

"You can spare me the indignant charade," Lettie quietly said. "I know about the photograph. Ghost aside, whoever set up that photograph intended to blackmail you with it."

Gwenna recoiled as if struck and closed her eyes. Lettie seized the opportunity to snatch the box of pills and was slipping it into her pocket when Gwenna opened her eyes and caught her. The transformation was impressive, from abject defensiveness to righteous offensiveness in a matter of seconds. "Just what do you think you're doing?" she demanded.

It was a terrible moment for Lettie, who blushed, suddenly feeling like a kid caught stealing apples. What would the Inspector think? But she recovered quickly, squaring her little shoulders and meeting her opponent's imperious glare. "I'm preventing you from taking any more of a dangerous, illegal drug," Lettie bravely answered.

Gwenna leapt up and snatched the box from Lettie's hand. "You meddlesome old fool!" she shouted. "You don't know what you're talking about. These pills were given to me by my doctor."

"That's what I was afraid of," Lettie replied. "How many have you taken?"

Gwenna narrowed her eyes and said, "I think you'd better get out of my house."

Lettie agreed, keeping her voice steady and trying not to take offense. After all, she was dealing with a sick woman, whom she'd just made feel intolerably vulnerable. A proud individual like Gwenna Hardcastle would naturally lash out in self-defense.

As Lettie left the room, Dame Gwenna's face sagged, suddenly looking like a well made-up corpse ready for the viewing.

14

THE INTERIOR OF THE CHÂTEAU was still, with the stale, airless atmosphere of a place barely lived in. The sparse but ornate furnishings were covered with a thin layer of dust. But there were a few signs of habitation—piles of magazines, an ashtray full of butts next to a wing-backed chair. Max reached under a tasselled lampshade and felt the globe of the reading lamp; it was still warm. In the hall an old pendulum clock made a steady sound, like snooker balls colliding again and again. Above him the ceiling creaked; old buildings had a tendency to settle—just another snip of data Max kept filed away under the category of "Spycraft—How to Break and Enter."

He silently crossed the room, testing the oak floor as he left the rug. The central hall was empty, save for a few suits of inferior armour, an umbrella stand, an armoire with a hazed mirror. He cracked open the door, saw a single raincoat, a pair of mud-caked boots. Chances were the house was under the not-too-thorough administration of some caretaker. One who smoked, read trashy French rags, and didn't clean his feet. The inside of this grand facade felt like a deteriorating ball and chain around some absentee owner's leg, a renovation that hadn't gotten under way.

Max knelt and pulled up his cuff, exposing a small Manlicher .25 caliber automatic taped to his calf. He pulled the tape back, involuntarily wincing as he depilated a section of his leg. He double-checked the magazine, sliding it in slowly against the catch to muffle the sound, then moved the safety forward, letting the weapon fit cosily into his palm.

He considered going up the stairs. Bedrooms, perhaps an upstairs study, a gallery; plenty of room to hide what he was looking for. But they could hide it anywhere—he'd told his superiors that. In the tip of a cane, hanging from Fido's neck, inside a perfume bottle.

But they weren't interested in his problems. Something of theirs had been stolen. Max had to find it. He remembered the blue van he'd just seen from the air, backed up to the other rear entrance of the building. Kitchen supplies, perhaps? He'd try there.

There was an extra door in the dining room. Judging from the cold, congealed debris on the plate set at the big table, the kitchen was nearby. He tiptoed up to the door, felt at the bottom edge for a draft, sniffed. In his line of work it was usually doors that got you. For one brief flash, you were a perfectly framed target, blind to what lay on the other side. He listened, his ears wide open, like a cat listening to an unfamiliar sound. Someone had recently eaten here, had probably been interrupted. By the van? The van would have a driver. Make it a minimum of two people in the house. No problem with those odds. As long as Max knew where they were. And there was only one way to find out. He pushed the door back, dreading the dry squeak of a hinge, but it didn't make a sound.

He found himself in the short connecting hall once used by the servants to bring dinner to the master of the house. The overhead bulb was out, but there was some light coming from around the corner. He gingerly slid his feet forward in the dimness, feeling for the unexpected carton, the crack in the lino. Reaching the corner, he held his gun up, next to his ear. A short flight of steps down, checkerboard tiles at the bottom, big black and white squares. The smell of wet coffee grounds, cooking oil, a hint of garbage.

Down the stairs, staying near the wall where the joists wouldn't creak. The kitchen was empty, dishes piled in the big carved stone sink. A blackened skillet sat on the crusty, black range. Checked curtains blew in the gentle wind coming through the open door at the far end. Between Max and the outside door was a pantry. He took a quick look. The larder was nearly bare, excepting a few tins of asparagus soup, pickled squid bits, an unidentifiable label of something that looked vaguely extraterrestrial. Max added it up: the caretaker seemed to be male, French, and a slob.

He drew aside the curtains with the barrel of his gun, saw the back of the delivery van just outside. He waited and listened. The gravelled drive was a mixed blessing. He would hear anyone coming yards away, or even somebody restlessly shifting his weight from one foot to another—even the best sentinels had to move sooner or later. But the gravel posed the same problem for Max, who wouldn't be able to move silently across it. And he had to look in the van.

He didn't move for a full two minutes, counting off the seconds with one small corner of his mind. Hearing nothing, he stepped out. He saw no one, but could now hear shouts coming from around the corner, presumably his Sloane chums struggling with their balloon.

He slipped into the back of the van and discovered five boxes, each the size of a coffin. Four were stacked up, a fifth had tumbled forward onto its edge. Judging from the fresh drag marks on the floor, there had been more; the off-loading had been temporarily halted.

He quickly looked over the boxes, noting the *carnet de passage* that had been stapled on each by French customs. They had all been opened and resealed with authentic tapes bearing the correct French imprints. All seemed in order. Customs wouldn't have let these through without a going over, not since Department had quietly passed word on to its French brethren. A bill of lading was taped onto each box, the usual data pertaining to shippers and jobbers. The point of origin was Portsmouth. Destination Marseilles and transhipment to a local drayage firm. All in order. In each box: athletic equipment. Specifically, something called Drongo Princess De-Luxe Chest Enhancers.

And that, Max thought, is something I've got to see. He began carefully to prise up a flap on the fallen carton.

Joey lounged back on the bed, puffing his fag down to his fingers as he lazily gazed towards the window. Through its open sash he heard the commotion below in the courtyard, even used a quantum of energy to take a quick look at the little balloon people scattered far and wee. It wasn't his problem; he was paid to drive a van and keep an eye on his cargo, not to run the bloody estate. He settled back on the bed and coughed. Nurse Fleming turned to smile over her shoulder, revealing generous curves under her filmy getup. She had the sort of attractions that would bring a man clear across the channel on foot; so he didn't mind getting paid to bring along a pile of clothes and gear for her recently acquired patient, who, she told him, looked like a living skeleton. He was glad his Nursie had some meat on her bones. She never would have to mess with one of those chest enhancers. Nursie got slowly out of bed and paced across the room like a lioness, took her turn staring out the window.

"Looks like Henri's in a dust-up with some swells who fell out of a hot air balloon," she remarked, adopting a maddeningly provocative pose that she'd worked on for hours in front of the mirror. Henri, that dirty little frog caretaker, Joey bitterly thought. Not half man enough for a red-blooded number like Nursie. Henri'd better keep mitts off, if he wanted to keep breathing.

"Let Ton Ton off his chain. That'll clear 'em off right enough." Joey pulled a last drag, reluctantly tossed his Player into a water tumbler. Ton Ton was another problem. Talk about nightmares—those eyes, that . . . that . . .

Something beeped, muffled but nearby. It took him a moment to recognise the alarm for his van beeping away in his pants pocket. Joey shot off the bed, ran across the room to where they were draped over the chair. "Damn! I told Henri to stay outta that van when I'm not there!"

Nurse Fleming looked confused. "But Henri's on the lawn down there. The van's in back, isn't it?" They stared at each other in horror. "Not . . ."

"Ton Ton," he grimly finished her thought. He jumped into his slacks, fumbled with his boots, the ones with the steel caps. He grabbed his jacket, squeezing the nine-inch length of lead pipe in his pocket. Here was the excuse he needed, catching Ton Ton red-handed, messing with the goods when nobody was looking. If he caught the monster by surprise, got in the first blow. Or better yet, "Where's that shotgun you told me about?"

"In the kitchen. But you'd better not hurt him! He's . . . well, you know whose man he is."

"Was, Nursie. Good as was. Ta." He was gone in a flash. Nurse Fleming looked at the open door, the unmade bed, the oily marks on the pillow, and sighed. This new job was like Siberia. Hardship duty. She ought to get extra pay. It was bad enough having to sit around for two weeks waiting for a patient who didn't even show up until last night. Now, at least, she'd have something to do. She shrugged off her negligee, padded barefoot towards the shower. Joey only showed up twice a week, but Ton Ton had made the time pass a little quicker. She was worried Joey was jealous enough to kill him. She'd hate to lose Ton Ton, for all his faults. There was something to be said for a big freak like him. She twisted the handle, smirked to herself as the water steamed out. But it couldn't be said in polite company.

Joey found the shotgun hidden in a drawer in the pantry. To his disappointment, he also found Ton Ton innocently cleaning his breakfast dishes. Grimacing at the nasty smell, Joey ordered the brute to come help him rout an intruder. As Joey slipped a cartridge into each barrel, he wondered just who the hell was playing around in his baby blue van.

The flap came away easily in Max's hand. He sniffed his wet fingers. The crumpled corner was damp on the inside. Some sort of fluid—machine oil, perhaps—had seeped into the cardboard. But it didn't smell like oil; it didn't smell at all. He opened the flaps the rest of the way, worked the contents out. The chest enhancer was a disappointment, just a frame of chromium tubes, this one bent in at one corner from the fall. Some sort of cam and gear arrangement with pads done up in stiff, silver-flaked polyvinyl. He eyed the damaged leg; the finish had partially chipped off, revealing ordinary steel underneath. He found the same oily film collecting around the plastic plug at the bottom of the leg. He worked the plug loose, and as it came away a small drop of clear liquid oozed out, liberally laced with shards of broken glass. He instantly realised this was what he'd been looking for. A vial of it had been concealed well up the leg of the appliance. It wouldn't show up on X ray, or in a quick visual inspection. And the chances of a customs agent probing every piece of tubing were small. The second realisation sank in as a tiny shard of glass bit into his finger. A drop of blood stood red against the clear fluid. The vile stuff would be in his system in minutes. Julia. Julia was his only hope.

Max jumped out of the vehicle, got only a few steps before falling hard as someone tripped him. He tucked his shoulder, using the momentum to carry him forward into a roll. He was back on his feet, bringing his gun up just a second too late. Joey, off balance from tripping Max, was on one knee next to the van. He had Max dead in his sights as he squeezed both triggers. The double barrels roared, rocking Joey backwards. Max dropped to the gravel as the gun went off. Lead shot whirred over his head as he sighted in on his assailant. Forced to fire while still in motion, he missed twice. The little slugs whanged into the open tailgate, making Joey dive behind the rear wheel.

Joey was frantically pulling shells out of his pocket when Max got to his feet and loomed over him. Joey looked up at the small barrel of Max's automatic pointing into his face. "Don't move, chum." Max didn't get a chance to say any more. A shadow fell across them; and Max instinctively juked to the left as a hatchet flashed past. It hit the side of the vehicle and carried through, the blade sparking and squealing a two-foot rent in the metal. Max pivoted on the balls of his feet, and found himself face to chest with a nightmare.

"Ton Ton! Kill him!" Joey screamed. Ton Ton was having trouble with his axe; his prosthesis couldn't grip the wooden handle properly. Sweat glistened on his plastic skull plate as he tried to figure out how to get his weapon free. Maybe if he just pulled very, very hard. The van rocked violently on its springs.

Max felt the first wave of nausea hit. Was he hallucinating already—or was he in the presence of the largest one-armed albino in the world? Max considered shooting this apparition just to be safe, but there were only six rounds in his clip. Six rounds wouldn't be enough to kill something that huge. Max opted for the oldest and most effective martial art he'd ever learned: He took to his heels.

But not to Julia, he thought as he raced through the kitchen, up the steps. Not with that ugly monster on the loose. And who was the gnome with the shotgun—the brute's keeper? Max dashed through the dining room, slipped and fell in the hall. He was getting weak, slightly dizzy. Only a few minutes left. To run? Never make it. Hide? Where? Max eyed the suit of armour and giggled. Fifteenth-century man had stood a foot too short. He heaved himself up with the last of his strength. If he could only make it to the closet. No, too obvious. He looked down. About a mile away were his chukka boots, right next to his gun. Silly of him to drop it. Need a parachute to float down that far. Such a long way. He thought he heard a thud, but was unconscious before it registered. It was the sound of his own body hitting the cold, hard floor.

15

JULIA WAS NONCHALANTLY sauntering in the direction of the château when Henri spotted her. His dispute with the snotty young English couple and their infernal balloon had eroded whatever good humour the little Frenchman possessed, which wasn't much, even when things were going his way. So he was even more vituperative with this new trespasser from the sky. There couldn't be many more, he nervously told himself; the basket wouldn't have been big enough.

Julia's almost total ignorance of French was probably an advantage. She understood very little of what the enraged Henri yelled at her, but gathered he wanted them to leave immediately. Babylegs made faces behind the caretaker's back, while Andy shouted above Henri's tirade, complaining to Julia that this silly little frog didn't speak English. Hostile sign language was getting to be a bore. And the damned balloon wouldn't ignite, no matter how much he fiddled with it. Something must have shaken loose in the landing.

Julia gesticulated, trying to convey her desire to use Henri's phone, saying in a combination of carefully enunciated English and halting French, "We can telephone our friends to pick us up and take the balloon away."

The conflict was still under way when a couple of rakish-looking gardeners putt-putted up the drive on dirt bikes. Parking a few yards away, they hung their berets and goggles on their handlebars, lit up cigarettes, and settled down to enjoy the show. Julia gathered from their shrugs that they didn't speak English either. The caretaker shouted at them, and the two reluctantly plodded off to work on the orchard.

Growing weary of looking into the Frenchman's open mouth and listening to his ceaseless harangue, Julia side-stepped him and made a dash for the back of the house, where she'd last seen Max.

She rounded the side of the building and arrived at the back in time to witness some activity at the tailgate of the blue van. A short, swarthy man and a grotesquely large, misshapen albino were shoving something into the cargo area. They were about to close the doors when an arm and hand dangled out the back. The arm was wearing Max's leather jacket.

"Max!" she yelled, instantly regretting such a reckless reaction when the stevedores looked up.

"Henri!" Joey yelled at the caretaker, who'd just appeared behind Julia. He pointed emphatically at her; but Henri ran past her, heading towards the van. He too had seen the arm and was as stunned as Julia. By the time Henri comprehended what Joey wanted and swung around to grab her, Julia was gone.

She sprinted across the gravel towards her fellow balloonists, working on a five-second message that would impress those two dim twits that Max was in mortal peril. She heard the van roar to life behind her, stones spattering against the château's walls as its wheels caught. In a few seconds they would be gone. She changed course, charging up to the gardeners' weather-beaten old Bultacos.

She'd driven a motorcycle before, when she dated a fellow who was a championship motorcross star, when he wasn't in a cast. She slipped on the goggles, pulled the thick beret over her hair and frantically tried to locate all the vital features. These things usually had a key; yes, there it was. Ignition on. Hold in the clutch, which is over here. Kick the lever down . . . there! It coughed hollowly like antique plumbing. She tried again, twisting the throttle grip. It hacked to life, with explosions popping in the muffler until it cleared its throat in a haze of unburnt lubricating oil. Now how did it go . . .

"Effing orf on a stolen bike, are we?" It was her dear friend Andy.

"Call Scotland Yard. Tell them Max has been kidnapped in a blue van," she yelled as she let out the clutch.

Andy blinked and shouted, "And where do I find a bloody phone?"

Julia shook her head, gave the bike too much gas and departed, front wheel skimming the ground. She belatedly remembered how to switch gears and, before Henri could try to tackle her, was well down the long driveway, the wind tearing at her light jacket. By God, it was just like a bicycle; once you ride one, you never forget.

She approached the road, saw the van turn left. She hit the rear brake, forgot the front one, and promptly dumped herself in the ditch next to the road. She picked herself up and savagely kicked the machine back to life, ignoring the pain that was zinging in her hands and knees.

It wasn't so hard, now that she'd gotten a better feel for the machine. It was light and responsive, and fairly stable as long as one maintained forward motion. She rode well back, keeping her quarry in sight as it travelled at exactly the speed limit on the narrow backroads. It was

Julia's intention to stay in contact until she could find a gendarme, or at least a call box. Although she couldn't remember if the French had police call boxes; all she could recall of French police was a toy-soldier image of pillbox hats with tiny brims, capes, and shiny black shoes.

Above the roar of air rushing past her face, she thought she heard a deeper drone than her motor's tinny racket. She anxiously looked down at the engine, hoping it wasn't about to self-destruct underneath her. Then she looked back to check her exhaust and saw the source of the noise: a genuine French policeman in blue serge and with a white helmet to match his white motorcycle. He frowned and forcefully signalled towards the verge.

She gladly pulled over. The cop expertly cut in ahead of her, deployed his sidestand and dismounted in one smooth motion. With studied nonchalance he removed his welder's-sized gloves and laid them carefully on his tank. He raised his goggles and circled her, exuding pomposity as he stroked his thin mustache. He noted the lack of a headlight, taillight, license plates. Incorrect tyres and illegal exhaust pipes. "Eh, mon vieux aviateur . . ." He pulled out his ticket book.

"Please, I don't have time for this. I need your help!" she impatiently began.

He looked up, surprised and gratified. A foreigner and a woman—wouldn't you know!

"My friend has been kidnapped in that van."

He surveyed the empty road ahead for a few seconds. "Eh. I see no *camion*. Now, your *carte*, if you please?"

Julia felt a momentary flush of anger. She wasn't going to let him waste her time while the crooks took Max away. She hadn't switched off her motor. She could just run out on this martinet and hope to find a more suitable policeman.

She shot forward, misjudged her distance and ran over the officer's perfect riding boots. He did a few undignified hops towards his BMW, deliberately pulled on his gloves as he sighted down the road towards his disappearing prey. So! It would be his 90 horsepower against the English girl's 30. It would be no contest! He started up and accelerated down the straightaway.

Someone was playing *Rigoletto* on a toy drum right next to Max's ear. Tat. Rat a tat tat. It began to fade in and out, making an interesting pulsating effect. He passed out.

Again he came to, aware now that the drumbeat was in his left ear, the one that was so cold. He tried to move, failed. His life story was swirling in his head. He felt like telling somebody about it—all the memories, secrets, the little creatures kept in a corner of his mind under a tarpaulin. He was ready to air everything out. More than ready!

Not *Rigoletto*. How silly. He was hearing the pitter-pat of tyres on pavement. The blue van, the mysterious, ever so interesting blue van. He was remotely aware of the chilly, corrugated floor, and that his hands were tied behind his back. That little sliver of glass had really put him in the ozone. Rather, what had been on the glass. Truth serum of the finest vintage. He really would enjoy telling some sympathetic listener all about himself.

He managed to roll on his back in search of a willing ear. A large white mound was staring at him. At least Max assumed that's what it was doing; it sat motionless, like something out of Madame Tussaud's. It looked like it had just washed up on the beach, or thawed out of an iceberg. Max wanted to tell the creature he was cute enough to work in a freakshow. Could he eat light bulbs?

But it all came out as a thick gargle; Max's tongue seemed to have been pickled in brine.

Ton Ton heard the noise and leaned forward slightly. He clicked his prosthetic appliance, like a giant lobster contemplating its prey.

"C'mere, handsome," Max mumbled. "Got sompin' to tell—" Ton Ton interrupted Max's life story by kicking out a long leg and slamming Max in the midsection with a size sixteen boot. Max subsided, gasping, listening to the roar of pavement, the creak of springs while he tried to hold his breakfast down. He was eventually able to begin again, "Now listen, I got to tell—" Max had to roll over again to evade another kick. Irritated, the albino got to his feet, braced himself against the side as he moved in on his victim, who was snivelling. "I can get you all the money you want. If you'll only— No, don't do that. Don't hurt me," Max whimpered as Ton Ton raised his heel over Max's head. Closer, handsome, just a little closer, Max thought to himself, acting fast as the gigantic heel came down. He kicked with his bound legs, cutting across the telephone-pole-sized leg that was supporting the albino's weight. Ton Ton swayed, but would have withstood the blow if the truck hadn't lurched over a frostheave. Ton Ton fell like a harvested oak. Max writhed out of the way, just avoiding being crushed.

Max decided to use his head, slamming his skull up under Ton Ton's prognathous jaw. There was a sickening crunch. The monster's jaw went slack, his eyes rolling up as whatever dim gleam of intelligence was there switched off. Max collapsed on top of his victim, laughing hysterically, feeling no pain from the growing lump on the top of his skull. "Come on, let's talk," Max said, nudging the big, misshapen head. Something told him he'd better stay hyped-up to counteract the jittery exhaustion that was sucking the air out of his lungs.

"Come on, what'sa matter—cat got your tongue?" Max heard his own voice, very far away. He was dizzy again, fading back out. Yawning below him, like some ivory-lined cavern, was Ton Ton's open maw. Max gazed into it and woke right back up. If the cat hadn't gotten it, somebody else had! No wonder Frankenstein here was such a sterling conversationalist! Max struggled to hold himself together, but a big squall came whistling across the van towards him. Dark, malevolent, pressing him down.

Damn the law and damn the consequences, Julia thought as she powered up to top speed. Just her luck to get pulled over by a mustache-twirling Nazi. Max's life was in danger and he wanted to write her a citation. Glancing over her shoulder, she nearly swerved off the pavement as she saw just how quickly the cop was making up ground. She held the throttle open for a corner, leaned into it while scanning the road ahead. A series of curves wound towards a gap between two low, rolling fields stubbled with mown hay. A sign indicated a junction was less than a kilometre away.

Perhaps she'd better not keep to the road. She slowed for an open gate in a hedgerow, turned in, and circled behind a low clump of willows. She heard the motorcycle moan past, then the squeal of brakes; he hadn't bought that trick. She wobbled away over the lumpy field, belatedly remembering to stand up on the footpegs. In a few moments she was among the trees, low shrubby things left by the farmers to provide cover for wild game. She gingerly worked her way down a cow trail. The Bultaco seemed particularly difficult to keep upright at this slow pace, and she was frequently forced to put a foot down.

Coming out of the thicket, Julia was relieved to see

relatively clear ground to the summit. But then she heard a crash not far behind her. Was it possible the cop could have navigated that field on his big, broad street bike? She accelerated, missed a gear, and turned to see her nemesis, his windshield hanging forward, shooting out dirt clods as he came after her. Waxed mustache or no, the ponce could ride!

Thigh muscles aching, she gamely stayed up on the pegs, like a jockey in the homestretch, as she headed for the top of the hill. She had to reach it, at least to see which road the van had taken at the intersection.

Julia's nerve might have failed her, had she known what lay just ahead. This particular plot of land had a hazardous anomaly. It had once been two parcels, separated by the usual Norman hedges: an earthen rampart on either side of a narrow lane, each verge topped by a thick stand of foliage. Then the lands had been combined and the hedges removed for the convenience of grazing cattle.

But the two ramparts, each the height of a man, remained. Their sides rounded by eight centuries of weather, hidden in the general slope of the hill, they were invisible. Until the last moment. She barely had time to gasp before the earth dropped away from her wheels. Her engine screamed madly. She instinctively leaned back, extending her legs. She flashed over the little roadbed some ten feet below, miraculously descending to earth on the downsloped side of the second pile of earth, which somewhat cushioned the impact. Throttle full open, she bounded twice and continued.

The French officer's skill was considerable. Despite the increasing heat of his temper, he rode coolly, scientifically. True, the passage through the trees had been tedious, but now, out in the open, he would surely—

The rest of that smug thought was lost forever as his

BMW became airborne. He responded perfectly, but the weight of a 900-cc motorcycle is three times that of a Spanish dirt bike. It landed like a crippled jumbo jet, the front suspension plowing in first, furrowing the dirt, spinning the motorcycle tailpipe over headlight. Various bits—radio, gas tank, mirrors—came spiraling off in their own trajectories. Including the pilot, who came to rest in a fuming heap, his breeches split at the seams, his helmet jammed over his nose. Only a steady stream of unscientific Gallic expletives arose from the smoking scene of the crash as Julia was up the hill and over.

16

By the time Lettie got home to St. Martin's Mere, the morning sun had gone from the garden, leaving her front porch in shadow. She unlocked the door, dropped her bag in the hall, and breathed deeply of the familiar scents of home—lavender soap, cedar, and lemon oil. The cottage seemed so empty without her terrier and housekeeper to greet her. She'd had to leave Tim with the neighbours, since Phyllis was still out on strike over that silly misunderstanding about the pistol.

Lettie turned on a few lights. What a relief to be back in her own cosily proportioned world only a few hours after Dame Gwenna had ordered her out. Perhaps the Hardcastle larger-than-life temper could be reduced if she'd get away from those fifteen-foot ceilings and stadium-sized rooms at Castleberry.

She went through the kitchen, putting on the kettle and ringing Mrs. Florie. Did she have time to come over for a cup of tea? Mrs. Florie said she did, obviously delighted to hear Lettie had returned. Lettie suspected some of that warm welcome might stem from the dear neighbour's eagerness to be rid of Tim. But Mrs. Florie insisted the dog had been an absolute joy . . . except for the evening she and her husband had gone out to play bridge. Apparently when they returned Tim wouldn't let them back into their own house. He'd turned into an absolute terror, so fierce and quick that he managed to keep them both at bay for an hour, until the fire company came. Such a good watchdog!

After her neighbour had gone, Lettie settled onto the couch in front of the fire, her dog (finally over the excitement of her homecoming) quietly lolling on the throw rug by her feet. For the hundredth time in the past two days, she wondered what could be keeping Julia. To take her mind off worrying, she spread the party photos out on the coffee table and sorted through them one more time, going over each with a magnifying glass until she nodded off. She had dozed for almost an hour when inspiration woke her. Hands shaking, she checked the pictures again to be certain, and found it to be true: there was no picture of Sam Gary entering the party, only one of him standing in the crowd after the body had been discovered.

Two quick calls convinced her she was onto something. She talked to both footmen at Castleberry, and both swore they'd let no one enter after the photographer had left the foyer at eight. Furthermore, all other means of entrance had definitely been locked; they had made certain of that. Whoever was at the party had to have come through the front door. She thanked them and asked for Bacon. She had left her number with him, but couldn't resist anxiously inquiring if there'd been any calls for her since she'd left. The butler assured her that there had been no calls, or he would have referred them to her home. She rang off with a frown. It really wasn't like Julia not to get in touch.

Quelling her increasing anxiety, she next dialled the offices of *The Sun* and got Montegue's emphatic assurances that no one could have gotten past him in the foyer without being photographed. He'd been instructed to get everyone who came in; and that's what he'd done.

She reviewed the party timetable once again. And this time proved the charm; the answer was there as plain as day. Sam Gary had come in the door, all right—the back door. When the diorama was brought in, he'd been hiding in or under it. And there he waited in the library until Freddie appeared. He'd somehow known Freddie would be there . . . She closed her eyes and reasoned it out. Sam Gary must have been abreast of Freddie's line-up of dirty tricks for the evening, because Sam was somehow connected to the whole campaign against Gwenna.

Sam must have remained hidden while Penny had it out with Freddie. After the girl had left, he came out from under the diorama and dragged the unconscious Freddie into the library. He was about to run Freddie through when he heard someone coming. He hid, and knocked out the intruder—so much for Max. Sam then hauled the still-breathing Freddie into the diorama and stabbed him to death. Ladling up some blood in a glass, he then returned to his hiding place under the diorama.

She closed her eyes and tried to envision the process. Getting a glassful of blood would have been a gruesomely messy business. He'd probably have had to wipe his hands and the outside of the glass clean. Perhaps with a handkerchief that he then tossed into the fire in the study? Yes, that would work. She thought about what must have happened next.

As soon as the diorama was brought into the darkened ballroom, Sam emerged, threw the blood on Gwenna, and shoved the glass into Cheever's hand. By the time the lights were back on the murderer was mingling with the crowd, as Montegue's candid shot recorded.

What details had she overlooked? Ah, the problem of fingerprints. Sam had no way of knowing Cheever would destroy them by dropping the glass into the alcoholic punch. Being clever, Sam would have taken precautions to avoid leaving his own prints on the glass. With another handkerchief or a pair of gloves, perhaps? Tucked innocently into his pocket, once he'd gotten rid of the telltale glass.

That was it, as neat as nine pins. Only the motive remained to be explained. She reviewed the information Penny had given her. Could the motive have had something to do with Freddie's impatience for the payoff, his plan to blackmail Gwenna? Freddie was becoming difficult to control, unreliable. He might queer the deal. So Freddie had to be eliminated, in a way that would further harass Gwenna—the final dirty trick.

It all seemed to fit. She agitatedly got up and roamed around her garden without seeing anything in front of her face. Something must be done to prove her theory, to put the villains away before they succeeded in destroying Gwenna too. And something had to be done about Julia. Lettie paced some more, then had an idea. She would call Colonel Thorn and have him contact his man watching Hoggwell. It stood to reason that Julia must be somewhere nearby; the Colonel's man could check on her welfare.

She was purposefully marching towards the phone when it started to jingle. Lettie answered it, collapsing gratefully into a chair when she heard her niece's voice.

"Sorry I haven't had a chance to make contact before now, Auntie," Julia breathlessly began. "No time to explain. Max is in trouble. I've followed his abductors to Godive, here in Marseilles. But I daren't try to get inside; they'd recognise me."

Knowing the sound of fear and exhaustion when she heard it, Lettie made her reply very casual, "Godive? Isn't that the name of the spa on the brochure you found at Sam Gary's?"

"That's right. I don't know who's inside. I was going to call the police, but thought better of it. Even if I could get through to them, it might be too risky sending them there. It could put Max in more danger . . . if he's still alive."

"Chin up. I'll call Colonel Thorn. He'll get Max out." When there was no reply, Lettie breezed on. "I should be able to get there some time this evening, depending on the plane. Where can I meet you?"

Julia named a hotel in Marseilles, said she'd keep watch outside Godive until eight o'clock, then would start periodically phoning the hotel to see if Lettie had arrived. She let out a deep sigh, promised to pull herself out of this funk, and added, "He just can't be dead."

Lettie delivered a few more words of encouragement and hung up with the distinct impression that Julia was in love with this Max, a very worrisome situation indeed, abductors and murderers aside. Her niece seemed to have a talent for falling in love with the wrong sort. Ah well, there was nothing for it but to get him rescued and hope for the best. She'd just give the Colonel a jingle; he'd have his man on the spot see to Max.

But it wasn't that simple. It turned out that Colonel Thorn hadn't heard from his operative in days. "I expect he'll be contacting us anytime, though. Who is this fellow they've nabbed?"

"I don't know much about him except his name—Max Genader."

There was a gurgling explosion, then the Colonel said, "Good God! *He*'s our man!"

Another piece of the puzzle fell together. Max had been investigating the Hoggwell and Sam Gary association, crashing Gwenna's party in the line of duty. At least Julia wasn't in love with some unsavoury character who crashed parties for thrills. That was some comfort. Although, being in love with a spy might not be much better.

"... A matter of departmental policy," the Colonel was saying. "I can't very well send in the troops after him; that might alert our pigeons before we've got them dead to rights. As for Genader, he's in a damned bloody position. We wouldn't want to do anything to put him more at risk. They could kill him in seconds."

"Oh dear," she groaned. "What should we do?"

"Let me think.... Problem is, that spa is the sort of operation that's difficult to get someone into without a great deal of preparation. And we don't have time for that."

She said she had an idea. If she could get inside, could he arrange for backup outside? "No! I forbid you!" he blustered. She brushed his objections aside; there wasn't time.

She made one more call before returning Tim to the reluctant care of Mrs. Florie and catching a taxi to the airport. Lady Katheryn Withers, the richest and most powerful woman in England, owed Lettie a small favour. It was time to collect.

17

GODIVE OCCUPIED ITS OWN exclusive niche, some thirty kilometres east of Marseilles. A niche carved out of the living rock of the Corniche. It was isolated from the road by a descending barrier and three miles of narrow, cliff-hanging drive. Creamy stucco walls and a young, alert staff insured that the unwanted didn't get in.

Lettie stood confronting a wrought iron gate set in the wall. Behind the gate a young man with long hair, a Godive T-shirt, and shorts was gently telling her that this was an exclusive club, a health spa. For members only. His slightly superior tone implied "for special people only." An old granny in a heavy coat, her glasses still frosted by the English autumn, was not that special. He turned on his heel to go.

"Young man. You misunderstand. I am not here as a guest." He looked back over his shoulder. "I am here to buy this property."

Peter Renton had been manager of Godive for only six weeks. It was a plum assignment, but then, he was a bit of a plum himself. Good-looking, tanned and fit, with just the right excess of curly hair and white teeth. He'd worked for plastic beads at Club Med, then graduated to running the bar of the Aloha Koa. He had charm, looks, and a ready smile. And he had that magic ability to flatten stomachs, lift bosoms, and smooth away crow's-feet with a smile and a wink.

He tried it on Lettie, rising from behind his slab of a desk, jaunty in flowered tropical shirt, light, form-fitting trousers, and sandals. "How do you do!"

"Very well." Lettie allowed him to take her heavy coat—it was rather warm after England.

"We're flattered you wish to stay with us, Miz . . ." Lettie looked vaguely around the room, and he continued. "You look so hale and hearty. And it's just as well. Your Guardian there—" he indicated the gatekeeper standing at ease next to the door—"has no doubt explained that we are a membership organization. I'm afraid it would be nearly a year before we could even consider an application. And we have very strict qualifications—"

"How much?" she asked, finally looking him right in the eye.

"I'm afraid our rates are, frankly, astronomical." He looked like that fact didn't keep him awake nights.

"No, no," she impatiently snapped. "For the property."

In confusion the manager looked at the gatekeeper, who all but twirled a finger next to his temple, saying, "She wants to buy the whole place."

Peter went back behind his desk and steepled his fingers as he fought back a smile. "My dear lady—"

"I am Lady Katheryn Tinsley-Withers," she informed him with a great deal of dignity. She hoped it wasn't too much.

This announcement brought Peter up straighter in his chair, as if the teacher had suddenly come into the room. It was hard not to react in such a way, in the presence of the woman who had, it was reputed, buried three of the richest husbands in England. She looked remarkably spry, the manager thought; that's how she must have outlived all those old boys.

"I require a piece of land. This is suitable."

The manager's face reflected the trains of thought that quickly rolled through his mind. "I'm afraid I can't help you in this matter. You must understand, I am only the manager. The owners must be consulted."

"Give me their names."

"I'm sorry, Lady Tinsley-Withers. I can't do that."

She negligently waved him off. "There is no need to burden me with petty details." She fixed him with a penetrating stare. "Do you know, young man, I have always gotten what I have set out to obtain. I can see you thinking, 'But this isn't England.' You also assume the owners don't wish to sell. I answer you with this." She reached into her bag for a folded slip of paper, handed it across to him and said, "That is the name of a certain minister in the French government. Below is another name that is very high up in this arrondissement. They wish to keep me happy—a matter of old favours. They will doubtless find a flaw in the title to this land, an error in one of your licences. It would be particularly interesting to examine *your* credentials as an alien worker in this country."

She continued to lay on the stoney stare, all the while inwardly amused at her own gall. The real Lady Tinsley-Withers had told her just what to do, called it throwing one's weight around. But would this colossal bluff work?

He tapped a finger on the desk, played with the piece of paper, and seemed to make up his mind as he snapped a finger at his staff member. "Guardian, bring Lady Tinsley-Withers some . . . tea?" He looked at her for affirmation. She nodded, quietly elated. My goodness, it had worked. Impersonating a lady worth three hundred million pounds did seem to open doors.

After tea was brought, Peter dismissed the Guardian. He poured for her, hitting just the right balance of deference and boyish charm. "You are quite a woman. When you came through that door, I saw some special quality, a depth of experience. A spark of . . . of . . ."

"My dear boy. I am not yet taking employment applications." She let a little tartness into her voice, then relented. Keep him off guard. "Although your cooperation in this acquisition would be appreciated."

He adeptly kept his balance. "I'm afraid my first loyalty must be to my employer." That was about right—don't sound like you'd cut your bosses' throats. Just stand by to change boats in midstream.

"I'm glad to hear that. I could possibly find a use for you."

He gratefully swallowed his tea, knowing he was over the hump.

"But you could do me one favour today, Peter." She smiled for the first time, and the fish took the fly without a second thought.

"Of course, dear lady, of course."

"I would like you to show me the property."

Lettie had to admit that if you wanted a place to eat yoghurt and dates, you couldn't do much better. Godive really was quite a spread: well over four acres of compound, walled on three sides and bordered by a steep cliff on the fourth. Protected from the winds, basking in the sun, the location was warm, quiet, perfect. Despite her mission, she couldn't help but admire the beautifully tended grounds with gardens full of blooming succulents, low palms, and bougainvillea vines clinging to the thick walls of the low bungalows. The staff Peter called "the Guardians," an Orwellian term if she'd ever heard one, were more plentiful then the guests. The few guests she saw were mostly middle-aged, lying by the pool and doing their best to acquire the breezy, tropical look, but most were still too pale.

The place didn't appear to be filled to capacity, as

she'd been led to believe. She remarked upon this while peering into an empty suite; she was already getting tired of thatched mats on walls. "Well, we're new," the manager answered. "It takes time to build up your reputation when you're catering to a certain calibre of clientele. You know, the stresses and strains leadership imposes can be subtly debilitating—that's what we're best at treating. We're designed to relieve the tension of those always in the public eye, never daring to let their guard down—"

"Thanks to the pariah dogs of the media," Lettie curtly dismissed the free press. "They make public life pure hell. That's why I've never allowed photographs or interviews."

"How wise," he cooed. "But not everyone has that luxury. Here we provide the opportunity to get away and unwind, while toning up. We maintain a full staff of therapists, counselors, and even medical personnel to meet every particular need."

Her ears perked up. "You have a medical facility?"

He nodded and pointed to a long building at the far end of the compound. Despite a stand of olive trees that broke up its slab sides, the structure had the indefinable aura of a clinic, mostly due to the high, narrow windows with discreet, decorative grating. There was a Guardian sitting at a table by the entrance, ostensibly weaving grass mats.

Lettie marched towards the building. The manager brushed past, lightly touching her arm. "I'm sorry, but we don't allow anyone in there. Some of our guests are in deep therapy and can't be disturbed."

When this made no impression, he said she surely understood that privacy was vital with these cases. She caught him up sharply, declaring that she never gossiped.

"You misunderstand," he protested in a hurt voice. "I only meant that with your tremendous social connections, you might actually know some of our patients—eh, guests," he finished lamely.

"I can assure you that none of *my* friends require any sort of higgery-piggery," she sniffed. "At least show me the outside of this hospital thing. I might be able to keep it for my orchids."

Her survey complete, Lettie allowed him to walk her to the gate. She requested a taxi; the gate Guardian left to make the call. "You're a most helpful young man," she told Peter. "I shall keep you in mind. You will please relay my interest to your employers."

"Of course."

"Excellent. Let me give you the name of my solicitors. Have you a pen and paper?" He went through his pockets, said he'd have to go get some, would be right back. This gave her more than enough time to use the device Colonel Thorn had given her to fiddle the lock. The manager returned and she wrote down the name of the firm Lady Tinsley-Withers had given her.

As the taxi drove her away, Lettie sat rigidly in the back, playing the dour old dowager to the hilt. But inside she was all smiles. Now all she had to do was coordinate phase two of the plan with Julia. They'd find out what really went on in the hospital facility behind that facade of tanning and tropical juice drinks!

Which reminded her. A break-in outfit would be required. She leaned forward. "Driver! Where can I buy a leisure suit and a straw hat?" The driver shrugged, but offered to stop and ask his wife.

18

MAX LAY QUIETLY ON HIS BED, his limbs immobilised by drugs as effective as any leather straps. He was clad in blue institutional pajamas. The only light in the room was from a reading lamp, which overwhelmed the faint wash of moonlight filtering through the high, grated window. Dr. Tony Hoggwell, sitting beside the bed, took his eyes off his patient when he heard footsteps approach in the corridor.

The door opened and Sam Gary crossed the room, stood at the foot of the bed. "This bugger and I already met. You give him the dope?"

Hoggwell pulled a towel off a stainless steel tray. "Just a light sedative."

"Why the bandage on the head?"

"Contusions from a fight with Ton Ton while they were bringing him down. That's why I waited a day to call you in. Couldn't use E-II right away and risk putting him in a coma. We'd lose our chance to pick his brain."

"We get through, I've got somethin' better than a coma." Sam prowled the room for a chair, then dragged it across the floor. He straddled it backwards and reached in his pocket for a smoke. "Let's get on with it. Full dose.

No beating around the bush, like we did with old Queenie."

The doctor unwrapped a syringe and snapped on a needle. He inserted it into the rubber cap of the vial, and held it up to the light as he carefully measured out the correct dosage. "With Gwenna we had to make it appear to be gradual mental deterioration. That was the whole point of my plan." A slight, smug smile appeared on his usually impassive face.

His partner snorted. "*Your* plan? Don't forget it was *my* bright idea to steal what keeps the muckety-mucks at the top—their smarts. Inside dope, military secrets, government policy. They sell better than diamonds on the open market, *if* you got the contacts. And *I* do!" Sometimes he was tempted to knock Dr. Know-it-all down a peg.

The doctor wrapped a piece of surgical tube around Max's arm and slapped the inside of his elbow to raise a vein. Sam looked into space as the needle slid in. "And who," Hoggwell irritably asked, "has the expertise to administer the treatments, to set up and run this place, and make the proper social contacts?" The single light glittered off his glasses as he looked at Sam. "Remember, it was one of my patients who got us access to this drug."

"After I put the squeeze on his family." Sam flicked cigarette ash on the floor. "But let's not get our hackles up. You've got your clinic and your fat clientele. And I get half of the proceeds from what we milk out of their whatsits."

"Subconscious," Hoggwell supplied, checking Max's pulse. "By the way, I think it's now safe to say that our plan has worked; Gwenna's quite susceptible now. With a little more E-II and a week's rest she'll be a goldmine of referrals. The perfect 'Before and After' advertisement. One week a total wreck, the next week back to normal and singing Godive's praises to all her well-placed contacts. We'll have only the very best, Sam. It'll be pick and choose, thanks to our Freddie's dedicated efforts." Hoggwell smiled. "And self-sacrifice. Too bad young Freddie wasn't a bit more patient."

Sam puffed, his face wreathed in smoke, his eyes squinted shut. "A Charlie gets in the way, then he don't."

There was the sound of light steps outside the door. It swung open and a little old lady in a straw hat and gaudy leisure suit peered at them through rose-tinted Vaurnets. "I heard voices," she meekly began. "Is this where I get my prescription?" She was looking at Sam Gary, who made an emphatic gesture to Hoggwell.

The doctor got hastily to his feet, automatically slipping into his bedside manner. "We're with a patient just now." He took her by the arm and tried to turn her away.

Gaping with unabashed interest at the prone figure on the bed, she asked what was wrong with that one there. "Gall bladder," Hoggwell promptly replied. "One of our staff."

"Big, isn't he?" she chirped, allowing herself to be hustled out into the corridor. Hoggwell briskly closed the door.

"Now, how can I help you?"

"I've just arrived, and I forgot to get a prescription before I left."

"What is it?"

She showed him an empty bottle. He read the label and promised to take care of it for her. The old lady smiled and sat down on a bench, as if to wait. "Oh, not just at the moment," Hoggwell explained. "I'll have them sent to your room, Miss Sledgewood," he said, reading the name off the pill bottle. "What room are you in?"

"I haven't the faintest. I just look for the orange bougainvillea vine and there I am! Now you go take care of that handsome young man's bladder," she told him, but he insisted on escorting her to the front door, making certain it latched after her. He glanced at the lock, unable to figure out how she'd gotten into the building.

Sam Gary was lifting up Max's eyelid. He let it drop as Hoggwell returned. "This one looks ready," he said.

"I'll be the judge of that," Hoggwell replied, brushing him aside to feel Max's pulse again. There was a beatific smile on the patient's face. "My dear fellow, how nice to see you again," the doctor cordially said in Max's ear. This elicited a smile of recognition from the patient, although his eyes remained closed. "We met at a party. Max, isn't it?" Max nodded, as Hoggwell kept up the chummy monologue. "The room was very warm, wasn't it? And the music quiet, like waves going in and out on a beach." At that last word the patient's smile expanded, as some particularly pleasant image rolled past his eyes. The doctor took this as a sign of progress. "Now, you can help me, Max, old man. I can't quite recall why you came to see me. You wanted to talk to me, right?"

"Followed you," Max chuckled.

"Why follow me? Is it part of some game? Who wants you to play this game, old man? Speak up."

"Sure." Max frowned, as if in thought. "Brown."

"Brown? Go on, I'm very interested."

"Brown. Father Brown. Capability Brown. Old Brown Study himself."

"What's that crap?" Gary asked in disgust.

Hoggwell hushed his partner up. "He's trying to fight it, go off on a tangent." To Max he said, "That's the man. But what's his real name? Your boss?"

Max's face contorted. His lips seemed to move of their own accord. "Section M . . . M . . . Division head . . ."

Max lapsed into mumbling as the lights went out. Hoggwell let out a curse. Sam Gary stumbled across his chair and thrashed for the light switch. It clicked to no avail. "Bloody power must be out."

He threw open the door; there was a little more light there, coming from the main compound, where the lights were still on. "Blew a fuse, looks like," Sam Gary said as Hoggwell bumped into him.

"The fuse box is down the hall, last door on the left in the broom closet."

"This is your clinic. You find it. It's too damned dark for me to go stumbling around."

"I can't leave the patient. He's ready to talk."

Sam Gary grumbled but set out down the hall, immediately crashing into a bench. He put together a string of curses when he rammed a wheelchair, but found it came in handy as he pushed it ahead of him, ruthlessly scarring the walls.

He was nearly to the end of the corridor when a ghostly apparition appeared ahead of him, the slim figure of a little old lady in a straw hat. The thin voice rang towards him. "I just remembered, I'd like those pills coated, please. Lemon flavoured."

Sam had had enough. "Lady, c'mere." She obediently approached. "You're an old snoop, aren't you, dearie?"

Her answer surprised him. "Yes, I suppose I am." There was a little chuckle in the dark. "And what are you going to do about it, Sam Gary?"

He reacted fast, shoving the wheelchair ahead of him, bouncing it off the walls at the end of the hall. He could just make out the one door the old bird could have gone into, and it just happened to be the closet he was looking for. Now he had her where he wanted her. He reached the door, grinned in the dark. As he stepped inside, he felt a shove in his back. Falling forward, he collided with a stack of brooms, put a foot in a box, lurched against the far wall and brought down an avalanche of linens that cascaded off a shelf. The door slammed and locked behind him.

Hoggwell could hardly fail to hear the commotion and was down the hall in a matter of moments, confident he knew where everything was located—until he felt a broomstick go between his ankles. He stumbled ahead, hit a waist-high steel tube and somersaulted forward into a laundry hamper. He struggled to free himself, letting out a yell when a heavy sack of dirty sheets smothered him. He felt another hit, then another. The cart whizzed down the corridor, rounded a corner, and stopped. He heard a metal lid lift, and felt the basket tip forward. The laundry chute! He fell into space.

The little old lady ran down the corridor, guided by a pocket flash. She threw her big hat off as she met her double coming around a corner. "Auntie!" Julia breathed.

"All went well?"

"Choreographed to a T. Where do we find Max?"

"This way." Lettie hustled into the right room. Julia directed her torch on his face, which looked badly battered, but was smiling dreamily.

She took his hand and smelled his breath. "He's been drugged."

"I'm almost out of oil, darling," he said, showing his beautiful teeth. "Roll over, I missed a spot."

"Oh dear," Lettie murmured. "I hope he can walk."

Max could, barely. Julia propped him up against the outside of the building while Lettie went ahead to scout. Max was shaking his head, breathing deeply the fresh night air, when he suddenly noticed Julia, who was holding him up. "Hullo," he said, wobbling on his feet.

"Keep your voice down," she hissed in his ear. He gave her a thumbs up. Lettie returned, indicating the coast was clear. Once through the gate their waiting car would speed them away into the night.

They would have made it, except for an unexpected roadblock. Rounding a clump of century plants, they ran into a much slower procession: a staff member perambulating one of the guests. All fell in a pile, Julia on top, feeling like a Mack Sennett comedienne. Something soft quivered in her face; it turned out to be a more-than-ample throat.

First on her feet, Julia helped her aunt up. From beneath the overturned chair, the attendant appeared, struggling free from the dead weight of none other than Dame Gwenna Hardcastle.

"Oh my God!" Julia moaned.

Gwenna was smiling in idiot delight, pointing at Lettie, who was busy straightening her clothes. "I know you," Gwenna babbled. "I know you." All traces of tension and fear were gone from her face, but then, so was any intelligence.

The attendant was staring suspiciously. "What is going on here?" he demanded.

Gwenna giggled. "Her name's Winterbottom. A meddling old snoop. Tried to turn me against my own doctor!"

The attendant looked at Lettie, then at Max and Julia. Here was a situation that would require some explaining. Fortunately, he was equipped with a small radio clipped to his pocket. He pushed the button, said, "The doctor, please." There was no reply. He changed channels and summoned all Guardians to the central courtyard. He clicked off and narrowed his eyes at Lettie. "Suppose you tell me what you're up to." Lettie began to hold forth, laying on her lady's arrogance, but it didn't work this time.

Not that it mattered. Julia had picked up Lettie's heavy, well-equipped handbag. She swung from the hip, laying it smartly against the enemy's temple, folding him up like a deflating concertina.

"Good job!" Lettie whispered as they ruefully contemplated Max and Gwenna, who were still in a heap, making silly noises. How to hurry two large, unsteady bodies?

With Max draped over Gwenna's lap, it took every ounce of both women's strength to push the wheelchair to their waiting car.

As seconds passed, Dr. Hoggwell managed to escape from the basement while his staff scurried about in confusion. Even as Lettie was belting their two passengers in, Sam Gary was being freed from the closet. And by the time Julia had started up their rented Peugeot Turbo, the barrier near the main highway was being dropped by remote control.

While Julia sped down the drive, Hoggwell and Sam Gary, automatic pistol in hand, were jumping into the spa's Mercedes limo. Julia negotiated the turns as fast as she dared, all too aware of the tremendous drop just a few feet beyond the verge.

"You're driving very well," Lettie encouraged from the back. She had placed herself between Gwenna and Max, who were swaying back and forth like twin lifeboats on a rolling deck. Julia could see their bobbing heads in her mirror and couldn't help but grin at the way they looked. She grinned too at the prospect of almost being home free after the awful uncertainty and physical exertion. Julia Carlisle, motorcross racer, and now champion rallye driver. Whoops! They were briefly airborne over a hump in the road. She easily corrected.

"Oh my," Lettie exclaimed, looking out the rear window. "I'm afraid they're following us!"

"No snag, lady, I'll shake 'em off," Julia replied, but her bravado faded when she rounded the last corner and spotted the length of steel pipe that blocked their escape onto the main road. She locked the brakes, knowing there was no hope of avoiding a smash as the tyres skidded. At the last moment she twitched the wheel, causing the empty passenger side to hit first. The barrier slid into the right side of the windscreen, smashing the glass and ripping out the doorpost. The car swivelled, metal screeching as the barrier bent up, caught where the windscreen would have been. Julia bounced off the roofliner and felt the shoulder strap catch hold on her chest.

There was silence, except for a ringing in her ears. She looked back and saw everyone in the rear compartment folded over like dolls. "All right, Auntie?" she shakily asked, staring at the headlights only a few curves back.

"Yes," came Lettie's quavering reply, as she pulled herself up straight and held her head. "What about you?"

"Still alive," Julia mumbled, dazedly pushing in the clutch. The engine caught immediately. She put it in gear and lurched forward a few inches. The tyres spun, the engine red-lining. She slammed it into reverse, trying to pull free of the pipe. The wheels spun; the car juddered and shook. The rear tyres got down to solid rock, and the car jerked backwards, pulling free from under the pipe.

And slammed into the front end of the Mercedes, which was just coming to a stop. The impact bounced the Peugeot forward with enough impact to knock the barrier up another fraction of an inch. Julia managed to change gears and squeeze under the barrier, the roof crinkling like a tin can. Then they were free, shooting onto the highway.

Sam Gary and Hoggwell hadn't bothered with seatbelts, so it took them valuable seconds to pull themselves out from under the dashboard. The impact had shattered their car's lenses and crumpled sheet metal. It had also bashed up the thug's nose and made him mad. He knew pumping a few rounds into the old bitch would make him feel much better. "They're getting away," he snarled. "Don't worry about scraping the roof—this thing's built like a tank."

Not bothering to answer, Hoggwell pressed the remote control button on the dash. The barrier raised completely up and out of the way.

Without a windscreen, Julia couldn't drive faster than sixty. In back, a hurricane gale brought Lettie back to her senses. "My word, what a ride! But we all seem to be in one piece," she bravely added, putting a hand on Julia's shoulder. Julia gave it a quick pat.

They were suddenly thrown forward by a thumping impact from behind. And another. Julia could only hang onto the wheel and pray she wouldn't lose traction. "It's them again," Lettie cried. Running without headlights, Hoggwell had still caught up! Again a bump, a vicious skid. Julia bit her lip as her headlamps swept out over space. They were horribly near the edge of the cliff, with the Mediterranean far below.

"Be ready on the brakes," she heard Max's voice in her ear and felt warm breath on the nape of her neck. She steadied as his hand clenched her shoulder. "Now!" he whispered. She stomped the brakes, locking up the tyres. Hoggwell, attempting to ram them again, was closing too fast. He made a desperate feint to the left and felt the long rear of the Mercedes come round. Next to him Sam was making a sound that rose in pitch. The steering became very light in his hand and he floated out of his seat, a deathgrip holding him to the wheel. *Sam's legs floated past his face* and then the impact seemed to rupture every cell in his body.

In the Peugeot, stopped just inches from the cliff, Lettie cried out as they heard a loud crump from below in the dark. Julia started to shake, allowing herself one racking sob, before backing up and driving on.

They were waiting for them around the next bend of

the highway: an Army lorry, gendarmerie, police cars, ambulance, a portable roadblock. Julia turned off the car and sat staring into the lights. A flashlight shone on her, then flicked to the back. She heard the voice of Colonel Thorn, as loud as ever, but with something extra behind those stentorian bellows. "Good show!" he shouted, opening the door for Julia.

"They went off the road back there," she dazedly told him, unable to find the energy to get out of the car.

He waved several police cars towards the cliff and said, "We heard the smash, dear girl. Were about to come take a look when you came up."

From the backseat Max cleared his throat, croaked, "Kraut cars never did handle," and fainted.

The physician took a look at Lettie and Julia and pronounced them both bruised but unharmed. Max was waiting in a stretcher, while Gwenna was taken off first, unhurt but comatose. Julia and Lettie were sipping something alcoholic that had been given to them by a French policeman. Several officers were shaking their heads and walking around what was left of the Peugeot. Max muttered incoherently from the stretcher. Julia asked if he was still under the truth serum. The Colonel thought he would be for several more hours at least.

"Then he's liable to tell the truth?" she asked.

A slight smile creased the Colonel's face. "As liable as he's ever likely to be."

Julia bent over, whispered a question in Max's ear. It took a few seconds. His eyes remained closed, but his face twitched. Then he said, "Yes." Julia stood up and grinned widely. In a few moments they were lifting his stretcher.

Colonel Thorn squinted at his agent as they put him into the ambulance. He wondered if Max *had* for once told the truth. And what was that look on Julia's face all about? Thorn hugged his two favourite women to his broad chest and said, "Your country owes you both a steak dinner."

"More than that," Lettie piped up, planting an affectionate kiss on his ruddy cheek. "It owes us an explanation."

A few hours later, over steak and truffles and a bottle of Burgundy, the Colonel filled them in on the developments. By that time, Hoggwell and Sam Gary's bodies had been recovered, and Thorn's men had gone through both the spa and the château near Giverny. They'd arrested Ton Ton and friends, impounding enough E-II to brainwash the House of Parliament.

"You mean they hired and coached Freddie to help drive Gwenna bonkers? So they could stage her miracle cure as an advertisement for their spa?" Julia tried to shake her head, but found her neck was too stiff.

"A lot of trouble," Lettie agreed, surreptitiously holding an ice cube from her waterglass against a painful bruise on her knee. "But it would have paid off. Dame Gwenna knows some prime potential brainwashing material. They would have been awfully impressed by her complete turnaround, thanks to a few weeks at Godive."

The Colonel explained that once the subject is taken off E-II, he remembers nothing. "In fact, the aftereffects are rather pleasant: One wakes up feeling relaxed and fit."

Julia asked what the museum project had to do with it. She slurred her words slightly, welcoming the numbing effect the wine was having on her badly bruised body. She felt like an entire rugby team had stampeded across her frame.

Lettie said that it was part of the villains' plan to make Gwenna totally dependent on her doctor. Hoggwell knew the museum was her fondest dream; so he got involved. As investors, he and Sam Gary could threaten to cancel the whole thing unless she went to the spa for a cure.

The meal and conversation came to an abrupt end when Julia fell asleep in her blancmange. Lettie remained chipper, if slightly drunk herself, buoyed up by the knowledge that her theories were correct.

As, indeed, they later proved to be. The Colonel's investigation, in concert with Inspector Alexander's work, found substantiation, the most convincing being minute traces of Freddie's blood on Sam Gary's formal shoes.

As for Gwenna, Norton Montegue told Lettie she was coming along nicely under the care of a decent physician. Lettie never heard from her—but that was to be expected. One didn't look up someone so closely associated with painful memories best forgotten. Benecia Hoggwell was eating regularly after an initial setback brought on by the shock of her husband's death and the revelation of his activities. Convinced she'd been unaware of the whole scheme, the authorities left the widow to recover in peace.

19

IT WAS A FEW DAYS LATER that Max got out of hospital. He put on the grey three-piece suit and striped tie that made him look like an unusually virile banker. He bought the most expensive champagne available and spent two hours locating a basket of ripe strawberries, the last of the crop imported from Spain. He showed up at Julia's door just as the sun was setting.

Dressed in her tattiest jeans and old flannel shirt, she was just finishing waxing the floor. She answered the door, took one look at the gorgeous man standing there and felt simultaneously annoyed and delighted. He could have called.

"Hullo, darling," he said warmly.

"Hullo. James Bond, isn't it?"

"May I come in?"

"Only a few steps. The floor is wet, you see." She moved aside and he came in. There was only a small area of floor that wasn't glistening with wet wax.

"You seem to be waxing yourself right out of the house," he said.

"Yes, I was just about to finish up, then go out for a sandwich and spend a few hours in the library until the floor dried."

"Surely we can think of some more amusing way to pass the time," he grinned, holding up the bottle. They were only a few feet apart. He pulled her closer, saying, "You saved my life. I like that in a woman." They laughed.

"Do you usually get into trouble like that?" she asked.

"Not usually. It was that damned drug that got me."

"Yes, I know." She gave him a tantalizingly secret smile. "Nothing like a little truth serum to help a girl find out where she stands."

He couldn't remember much from that night, certainly nothing about confessing to being in love with her, which he had, of course.

"How long have you been in the spy business?" she asked, meeting his warm look with one of her own. He almost dropped his bottle of champagne.

He kissed her mouth and said, "Why don't we continue this conversation at my flat? The floor is dry and the sheets are clean. There's a steak in the fridge and a 007 flick on at nine."

"I hope it's *The Spy Who Loved Me*," she replied.